Everything To Lose

A Lucas Holt Novel
Book One

By JP Ratto

EVERYTHING TO LOSE

Limitless Publishing, LLC
Kailua, HI 96734
www.limitlesspublishing.com

Formatting: Limitless Publishing

ISBN-13: 978-1-68058-421-9
ISBN-10: 1-68058-421-9

DEDICATION

For Andy and Katie.
Our most successful collaboration.

CHAPTER 1

The woman in the sunburst yellow dress settled behind a small boy who stood between his parents in the front row. In her carefully chosen spot, she would have no problem seeing the senator. More important, he would be able to see her.

Following the presidential candidate's schedule occupied most of her time. She knew him, and his routines. He was a clever politician, a clever man. At one time, she admired that about him. In spite of his womanizing history, she'd held him in high esteem. She hadn't cared about the rumors of his less-than-ethical political acumen. He was bright and confident. Like her, he knew what he wanted and achieved it. The one thing he lacked was loyalty. That was his one unforgivable flaw.

A momentary stab of rejection cut through her as crushing memories of betrayal clamored to the forefront of her mind. Another staunch memory held them at bay, protecting her as always from thoughts that could leave her filled with rage or shattered from distress. *I did what I had to. He gave me no choice.*

***

Rows of supporters without access to the ticket-only event stood shoulder to shoulder, necks stretched and ready for a coveted glimpse of the man who could be the next president of the United States. Young and old mingled together, most dressed in patriotic colors and wearing **'Grayson for President'** buttons. Tabloid reporters and photographers took strategic positions at the iron-gated entrance to the prestigious institution.

The mainstream press had already set up their sound and video equipment on Columbia University's south lawn. Amsterdam Avenue was closed for two blocks north and south of 116th Street. With the absence of through traffic, the cacophony of city activity hummed in the distance. Escalating murmurs obscured the honking horns, worn, grinding transmissions, and truck trailers loaded with goods booming as they slammed into the streets' deep potholes. Area residents, intent on going elsewhere, glanced at the restless group and at the clouded sky. Briefcases and umbrellas in hand, they hurried to subway stations or Columbus Ave to hail a cab.

***

She'd been waiting for the event to begin since spectators and press had started to arrive. Turning toward the reporters at the campus entrance, she caught a brief glance from one of them. She almost shook her head in reproof when he gave her a slight nod. Instead, she ignored his acknowledgement and vowed not to look his way again.

She checked her phone for the time. It was still early, but she could be patient. Another half hour was nothing compared to the years she'd waited for what she deserved, or rather, what *he* deserved.

***

As if on cue, stubborn puffs overhead gave way to a glorious blue sky on the warm August afternoon. Mounting shouts and whistles alerted all to the arrival of a line of black vehicles crawling at the curb north of the entrance. Men and women clothed in dark suits, more apt for a funeral than a summer outdoor event, exited onto the street. With serious faces, they scrambled to organize their positions before the guest of honor emerged. By all the staff and security Senator Grayson utilized, one would think he'd already won the election. Some criticized his self-importance. Those who knew him well commended his prudence.

All who gathered cheered as presidential candidate Senator Todd Grayson exited one of the limousines. Skilled at working a crowd to his full advantage, Grayson took his time. Straightening to his full height, he smoothed the jacket of his lightweight, ivory linen suit. He looked like a white knight among his entourage of black-clad minions. He faced the street audience, threw up his hands, and waved.

A mass of hand-held banners and American flags flapped like a flock of gulls vying for a prized clam. Classically tall, dark, and handsome, he had as many men fawning over him as he had women. Not since JFK had a presidential candidate charmed a constituency as Grayson had.

Grayson's staff paved the way for him to enter the campus, shielding him from direct contact with those crammed behind the barricades. In a move that was either spontaneous or a well-contrived plan, the senator turned and walked in the opposite direction and began to shake peoples' hands. The crowd went wild with whoops and shouts for attention. Surrounded by his campaign staff, his personal counsel Douglas Cain, and his bodyguards, he navigated among potential voters like a rock star.

Grayson stretched over the wooden barriers grasping as many hands as he could. Men removed their caps in respect, nodded, and returned strong, steady shakes. Women squealed and clapped, some patting their beating hearts as if they might swoon. His broad smile bared perfect white teeth that contrasted with his golden skin. Grayson's careful choice of attire, including the pale blue shirt and tie, conveyed the tranquility of sand and sea. You could hear sighs of contentment at Grayson's touch.

As president, Todd Grayson would take care of you.

He moved to the end of the narrow walk and back again toward the campus, scanning the adoring crowd. Grayson slowed when he noticed a woman who appeared oblivious to the lively throng surrounding her. She stood still but for a subtle bob and sway, like a buoy when bumped by gentle ocean swells. Tall, with shoulder-length blonde hair, her bright yellow, sleeveless dress set her apart from all the red, white, and blue. Her white designer handbag hung on her shoulder and she clasped her hands low in front of her. Grayson watched her lift her hand to adjust her dark sunglasses. Sharp and adept at reading people, her stance unnerved him. He couldn't see her eyes, but he sensed her stare. He would have thought she was blind except her head turned to follow his movement.

Douglas Cain nudged the senator's arm, breaking the connection with the woman. "We need to move along, Senator, if we want to keep to the schedule."

"I know, Douglas, but this is as important as a stump speech," Grayson said, his practiced smile never leaving his face.

Cain had been with Todd Grayson from the start of the senator's venture into politics. With Grayson's reputation and past, his lawyer's presence at all functions was paramount. About to enter the campus, where another group awaited the senator's appearance, one of the tabloid reporters caught Grayson's attention.

"Senator, you look well rested from your vacation in the Hamptons. What is your response to some of the negative pushback by your opponent regarding your position on defense spending?"

Grayson glanced at the reporter's nametag. "Tom, it's not my policy to waste time on the defensive—at least not until the debates. I'll continue to do what I've always done, and that's to present my ideas directly to the people. It's the folks' opinions that count."

Those standing nearby nodded and applauded their approval. Before Grayson could turn away, the reporter asked another question. "Senator, is it true that you were involved with call girl Sheila Rand and were a prime suspect in her murder?"

Grayson did not move. The rapid blinking of his eyes as he processed the question was the only indication he had not turned to stone. *Sheila Rand.*

He had not thought of the woman for sixteen years. It was true they'd had a brief affair, but he'd had an alibi for when she was murdered. Cain had taken care of it. He'd taken care of that and another matter.

A moment of recognition flashed through the senator's mind. He whipped his head toward the woman in the yellow dress. A stream of perspiration dripped down his face as he desperately searched the crowd. *Where is she? Was it her?*

"Senator?" the reporter prompted Grayson.

Grayson eyed the reporter. Cain moved in to stand between them, but Grayson refused to be intimidated. He grinned.

"Tom, you need to check your facts before you ask questions that make you look foolish. I have nothing to hide. Sorry, but I'm on a tight schedule," he said and allowed Cain to guide him away.

A grin still pasted to his face, Grayson's thoughts swam with dredged-up memories of the past. His chest filled with anxiety. He couldn't breathe. Grayson was drowning in thoughts of all that could go wrong. He looked at Cain, his protector—his life preserver. He exhaled a breath he hadn't realized he'd been holding. The lawyer would deal with any fallout. That was his job.

Grayson shook off his concern and strode through the university's gate to where he would give a rousing speech. Excited college students and faculty packed the stands. They applauded as he stepped to the podium. Another stage. Another performance. Everyone quieted and Grayson began the prepared rhetoric he knew would raise spirits and hopes. That was *his* job.

As his popularity tide rose, Senator Todd Grayson glided into the hearts and minds of those who would elect him to the most powerful position in the world. It would be smooth sailing, unless the long-ago matter of a murdered call girl surfaced and dragged his political career into a maelstrom of disaster.

CHAPTER 2

Sitting on my usual stool, I scanned the menu scrawled on the chalkboard suspended over the bar.

"I'll have the cheeseburger and fries, medium rare—and hold the onions," I told Kyle, the bartender.

"Great choice, Mr. H., coming right up."

There wasn't much choice from the limited menu, but I didn't go there for fancy dining. I was there to meet someone. I had come home from my workout at the gym and noticed a note shoved under my door. It took me by surprise. With all the high-tech ways to connect, passing a note was at the bottom of the list. The message was to the point.

McAllister's, Thursday, 2:00 p.m.

That's it. I should have thrown the summons in the garbage, but the paper was expensive and the handwriting feminine. I admit I was curious. For one thing, why bother leaving me the note at all. I'm in McAllister's Ale House at least three times a week. It would've been easy enough to join me at the bar on any one of those days. I figured this person didn't want to wait for a chance meeting and didn't want to use her phone.

McAllister's is a fifteen-minute walk from my Gramercy Park townhouse. The quaint pub boasts a dark, rich environment, loaded with memorabilia dating back to the eighteen hundreds. Parked on a barstool where Teddy Roosevelt or even Abe Lincoln might have sat is humbling and allows me to forget some of my modern-day problems.

"Here you go, Mr. H., medium-rare, no onions." Kyle set my lunch on the bar along with a mug of beer. Patrons are encouraged to order any beer they like as long as it's McAllister's pale ale or dark porter.

Before I could bite into my burger, a woman sat on the next stool. I could feel her eyes on me and glanced at my phone. If it was my "date," she was early.

"Excuse me," she said.

The young woman appeared to be in her late twenties, had long black hair, and exotic dark eyes. I smiled.

"Yes?" I asked. She smiled back. I waited. Since I didn't know whom I was meeting, I wanted her to introduce herself first.

"Did anyone ever tell you that you look just like the actor who played Two-Face? Can't think of his name, though."

In spite of wondering what I'd gotten myself into if she was the one who left me the note, I couldn't resist asking, "Which of the two faces do I look like?"

She laughed. "Oh, before the explosion, for sure. Wait, I remember. Aaron. Aaron Eckhart."

"Really?" I mentally compared myself to Mr. Eckhart.

"Yeah. You have the same sandy-brown hair and that sexy cleft in your chin. You seem tall. How tall are you?"

"Six three." It felt like an interview, and I didn't know why I was answering her questions.

"You even have blue eyes. I'm pretty sure his eyes are blue. You aren't him are you?"

She continued to study my face as my hamburger was getting cold. Clearly, she was not the one who left me the note.

"No." I grinned and thanked her for the compliment. "I don't mean to be rude, but I need to finish my lunch. I have a business meeting with someone in a half hour."

She frowned but took the hint. I supposed comparing men to actors was her way of breaking the ice with those she wanted to get to know. I was flattered, but I wasn't in the market. At least not that day. She stood, giving me the opportunity to assess some of her fine physical attributes. She gave me a wry smile that seemed to say, "Your loss."

"Sorry," I said, and I meant it. She left the bar.

At 2:00 p.m. on a weekday, the place was still full with the lunch regulars. When a table opened up, I took my mug and sat down. I didn't have long to wait before a woman, who looked familiar, entered the pub.

Blonde and statuesque, she wore a waist-length

navy cardigan with pleated cuffs and hem, over a white dress. My ex-wife Susan had a penchant for expensive clothes and often described to me the "perfect little jacket" she'd seen or the "most adorable pair of shoes." I'd had to learn fashion terms to understand what she was saying.

The woman's makeup was natural, not heavily applied as some her age tend to do. I guessed she was in her forties. She was well put together and totally out of place in McAllister's. If she was here for a clandestine meeting, she'd chosen the wrong venue.

She scanned the crowd, her eyes widened with recognition, and she strode with purpose to where I sat.

"Lucas Holt?"

"That's me." I stood and indicated the empty seat across from me.

She sat down, placed her purse in her lap, and leaned forward, hands clasped on the table. Her body language was all business. I waited for her to start the meeting.

"Mr. Holt, thank you for coming. My name is Janet Maxwell, and I need your help."

I took a few seconds to process her name. Maxwell was the name of a private investment company in the Big Apple, one I'd checked out to handle my personal finances, but went with one of the big-name firms instead. I remembered seeing a recent blurb about the company in *Investor's Business Daily*, some trouble with the management. Janet Maxwell's clothing and manner told me she was educated and had means. I doubted she was there to solicit financial business.

"Would you like something to eat or drink, Mrs. Maxwell?"

She hesitated and took a deep fortifying breath. "I could do with a glass of wine. Chardonnay, please."

I signaled for a waiter and ordered. We engaged in idle chitchat about the history of McAllister's until the drink arrived.

"What made you so sure I wouldn't throw away the note?" I asked.

"I hoped you wouldn't. I'm reluctant to use my phone these days. Conversations are not always private. What I have to discuss must be kept between us."

"How do you know me and what I do? I assume you're here to ask for my particular professional services."

"I first heard of you when you were with the NYPD. You worked on a murder case involving an acquaintance of mine. I followed the progress in the papers."

I knew the case. It was one I've struggled to put behind me but stubbornly remained at the forefront of my mind. I realized how I'd known the woman who sat across from me—from the newspapers. Her husband, president of Maxwell Investments, and their ten-year-old son died in an automobile accident. I wondered why she was asking for my help. Did she think their deaths weren't an accident? I'm a private investigator, but at the time, my focus was to locate kidnap victims.

"Mrs. Maxwell, what is this about?"

Her eyes glazed with tears and she looked at me with pity. "I'm so sorry about what happened to your daughter, Mr. Holt. I can fully imagine your pain."

My pain. The unimaginable pain I endured fifteen years ago has become a sort of dull ache. Except when someone forces me to relive the horror by bringing up the incident and telling me how "so sorry" they are. At that moment, I regretted being there; I should have burned the damned note. This woman knew a lot more about me than I did about her. I waited for the stabbing in my gut to subside and took a large swig of my ale. My jaw clenched.

"How do you think I can help you, Mrs. Maxwell?"

My tone was colder than I intended, and she jerked back in her seat. I saw a fleeting look of anguish and futility pass over her face, as if I'd already refused to help before she could persuade me I had to. She took a moment to recover, her eyes never leaving mine. This was a woman with resolve. Her expression softened, and I hoped to God she wasn't going to tell me, again, how sorry she was for my loss. She opened her handbag, pulled out a photo, and held it out to me.

"Mr. Holt, I need you to find my daughter."

I picked up the photo.

Three girls in their early teens posed in front of a covered bridge. I did the math. "Is this your daughter in the middle?" I could see a resemblance.

"Yes."

"Is she from a previous marriage?"

"No, I was never married to the father."

Up until now, Janet Maxwell appeared in control of her emotions, considering her recent tragic loss. But just the mention of the father seemed to rattle her. She slouched in her chair, tugged at the bottom of her sweater, and twisted her hands in her lap.

"Did you have custody of your daughter?"

"No, I never did." She picked up the napkin from the table and dabbed her eyes. "I gave her up for adoption."

"This photo is evidence you've had contact with her before."

"Not directly. The lawyer who handled the adoption kept me informed of her progress through life—sent me pictures. It was part of the arrangement."

"That's a pretty favorable deal. But you never had personal contact?"

"No, it was not part of the arrangement. My daughter doesn't know who I am. That's why I'd like you to find her."

"What about the lawyer? Can't you go to him? Revise the arrangement—your daughter is how old?"

"Seventeen. She'll be entering college in the fall. That's the last photo I have of her."

"Then she's a grown woman. This lawyer should be able to help you."

"He won't help me. He told me two years ago he'd lost contact with her adoptive parents and is not sure where she is. The family moved and left no forwarding address."

I pushed the photo across the table. "Mrs. Maxwell this isn't my area."

"Please, Mr. Holt." Her eyes watered and her voice was a whisper.

I'm not a hard case, and I hated turning her away. With her social connections and money, I was sure she could hire the right person for the job—it just wasn't me.

"If the lawyer won't help, then there are investigators who are in business to locate birth parents and children. You'd be better served hiring one of them."

"That's not what this is."

I could sense there was something she wasn't telling me. Her eyes had held such fortitude when she first sat down. Now, they averted mine and focused on the diamond ring on her finger, which she pulled on nervously.

Only a few patrons remained at the bar. The tables all around us were cleared and reset for dinner. I glanced at my cell phone for the time. We'd been there for over an hour, and if I didn't move the conversation along, we'd be there all night.

"I'm sorry, but you've not given me enough reason to take this case."

She closed her eyes and sighed deeply. Not quite a resignation, but she knew she had to give me more if she wanted my help.

"I didn't want to give up my daughter, Mr. Holt. They forced me to do it. Then I moved on, got married, and had my son." Her voice cracked, her grief coming to the surface. She took another deep breath and continued.

"My daughter is the product of an affair I had

15

with a married man who was and is a prominent figure. Once I told him I was pregnant, he refused to see me again and cut off all direct communication. He sent his lawyer to assure me I would be financially compensated. He gave me details of a plan to either terminate the pregnancy or agree to adoption. I chose the latter, hoping for a way to raise the child myself. But I was so closely watched and constantly reminded of my obligation and the dire consequences if I did not comply."

Janet Maxwell's manner vacillated between bravado and fear. The conversation would appear strained to a casual observer, so I flagged the waiter and ordered a couple of drinks and an appetizer. A few early birds entered the pub for dinner and, luckily, sat far enough away to afford us privacy. The case of Maxwell's missing daughter grew more and more intriguing. This was not a simple case of paying hush money or making things right. This sounded like coercion. If I wanted to parse the situation, I'd liken it to a kidnapping.

"Consequences?" I asked, picking up where we left off. "You were threatened—how?"

"At the time, my parents were alive, and I believed they would come to some harm if I didn't do exactly what I was told. Then after I married, the threat extended to my husband and son. Now, it's just me."

"Has someone threatened you recently?"

"Since the birth of my daughter, my life has always been in danger. Think of the scandal if my relationship with the father is revealed."

"You need to tell me who he is."

She sat straight up in the chair, tucked her shoulder-length hair behind her ears, then placed her clasped hands on the table again—an obvious attempt at composure.

"I'd rather leave him out of it. It has no bearing on locating my daughter. Her father chose to be out of the picture from day one. To the best of my knowledge, he's conveniently forgotten she exists. Still, I want to know where she is, so if necessary, I can protect her."

"You believe she's in danger."

"I believe we both are."

I leaned back in my chair to digest her statement. I wondered if she was telling me the truth. Or was she telling me what I needed to hear so I'd agree to find her daughter?

"Do you believe the lawyer has lost contact with your daughter?"

"I believe that if he's lied to me and knows where she is, then her life is as much at risk as mine. I hope and pray someday I will see her again."

Those words hit me hard. I could've uttered them myself. They'd passed through my mind every day for the last fifteen years. It was my turn to compose myself.

We both took a much-needed gulp of our drinks. The appetizer lay untouched. Janet Maxwell feared for her life. Whether she searched for her daughter or not, she was a loose end. With Maxwell's family dead, the principals involved in this arrangement had nothing to keep her from divulging their secret—except for the daughter.

I was ninety-nine percent certain I would take the case. My decision hinged on one more piece of information.

"Mrs. Maxwell, I need to ask you again, who is the father?"

I was taken aback when Janet Maxwell's grim expression left her face, replaced by a brilliant smile that revealed expensive porcelain veneers. The resilience was back in her eyes. For a fleeting moment, I thought I might have been the subject of a hoax. She sipped the last of her wine before answering.

"Mr. Holt, the father is Senator Todd Grayson."

CHAPTER 3

After what she told me, I had suspected who the father of her child was. When Janet Maxwell said she knew me from an NYPD case I had worked on involving an acquaintance of hers, I knew it was the Sheila Rand case. I don't do murder anymore—not if I can help it. Her family was dead and there was nothing I could do. I had been all set to refuse to help this woman, so the less she told me, the better.

Then she mentioned my daughter.

I wanted to bolt from the seat, run home, and boost the slight buzz I had going with a bottle of scotch. It took all my mental strength to keep focused on Maxwell and her story. The parallel was uncanny except she played an active part in the disappearance of her daughter. Well, maybe I did too. The bottom line was the same; we both lost a child for the sole purpose of covering somebody's ass.

I first became acquainted with Grayson working as a detective, second grade at the twelfth precinct in lower Manhattan. My partner Ray Scully and I picked up a case to investigate the possible homicide of a call girl found in a Bowery apartment.

Normally we wouldn't expand our search for suspects beyond the local residents and sex offenders in our system, but at the time the area, known for its flophouses at the turn of the century and famous "skid row," had begun a gentrification. Renovated, swanky apartments attracted a few high and mighty and some who thought they were. Todd Grayson, Junior Senator was one of the latter. Cocky and snide off-camera, his dabbling in the unconventional was whispered about in New York high society. Preliminary evidence and a not-so-credible witness led us to the senator. My partner and I visited his office to ascertain his alibi and rule him out. It was routine to follow all leads. Todd Grayson was not available, but his secretary checked his calendar and told us he had been out of town at the time of the girl's death.

Before we could verify Grayson's alibi, there was immediate pushback from the brass and political circles to ignore the lead and turn the investigation to a more appropriate suspect. Our captain strongly suggested Scully and I not question the senator.

The more evidence we gathered, the more it looked as if Grayson might be involved, directly or indirectly. We had our orders—but being a staunch proponent of justice, I couldn't let it go. In hindsight, I ask myself, why not. I ask myself the question every day. But hindsight is worthless. My instincts were dulled by a determination to see justice served.

Ray, my partner and friend, had the sagacity to leave it alone and did his best to persuade me to do the same, to no avail. Two weeks later, my six-month-old daughter was abducted from a day care center. There was never a demand for ransom. At the time, I thought it a random act by some disturbed person—someone who wanted a child, not money. After the incident, the day care center burned down. The owner died, cause of death inconclusive.

An exhaustive eight-week investigation and search turned up no trace of Marnie. I don't know how I lasted six months more on the force. I left to devote all my time to finding my daughter. A year after the kidnapping—after living with a woman who I knew blamed me but never said it aloud—my wife Susan and I divorced.

For as long as I remembered, I always believed Todd Grayson was in some way responsible for the death of that call girl and for the kidnapping of my child. I thought taking the Maxwell case might be a way to prove it.

"So, Mr. Holt, have I convinced you?"

The sound of her voice startled me. It must have taken only a few seconds for my past to flash through my mind.

"Convinced me?" I asked to give myself more time to settle back in the present.

"Yes, to find my daughter." She pulled a checkbook from her wallet. "How much do you want as a retainer? Would ten thousand be enough?"

Janet Maxwell was all business again. I sat there staring at her, wondering whether I would take this case for her benefit or mine. Did it matter?

"I can't guarantee I'll be able to find her, Mrs. Maxwell. I'm still not sure I'm the right person."

"Mr. Holt, what else can I say to persuade you to help me...and possibly yourself?"

Shrewd. Janet Maxwell was beginning to resemble a chameleon. She could change her persona to suit the circumstance. Something about her troubled me. She had done her homework. She knew all the chinks in my armor. I wondered if I could trust her. My face must have given me away.

"You don't trust me, do you? You think I've been less than honest with you. Well, you're right."

I noticed her eyes were the same deep blue as the tear-shaped pendant she wore around her neck. She manipulated the stone between two fingers as she spoke. I found the action almost erotic.

"Am I?" I asked in another maneuver to collect my thoughts.

"I see you need more incentive."

"What haven't you told me, Mrs. Maxwell?"

Janet Maxwell's smug expression was all the preparation I needed for what was to come.

"I have first-hand knowledge of Todd Grayson's relationship with that murdered call girl."

CHAPTER 4

In his plush leather and mahogany office, Douglas A. Cain, Esquire gripped the arms of his executive chair until his fingers cramped and his knuckles turned white.

Cain tried to concentrate on the brief in front of him. Someone had brought suit against a Grayson family member. The wealthy were often a target for frivolous lawsuits, the latest a particular nuisance, and waste of his time. *Son of a bitch, I don't have time for this.* He slammed the file shut and shoved it away.

Douglas Cain rose from his desk and paced his office.

He had provided legal counsel to U.S. Senator Todd Grayson even before the young politician's election to junior senator representing the state of New York. He and Grayson had both received their law degrees from Yale. Cain had the brains and Grayson the money and connections necessary to attend the prestigious law school. The two men had an immediate rapport. Cain's pale skin, fair hair, and hazel eyes, hidden behind metal-framed glasses, rendered him invisible next to Grayson's dark good looks. That suited both of them.

Cain began his career as Todd Grayson's handler in their second semester when one of Grayson's indiscretions nearly caused his expulsion from the university. Also at stake was his engagement to the daughter of a respected business acquaintance of his father. The marriage would guarantee Todd Grayson easy access to political connections in New York.

With his friend's consent, Douglas Cain had persuaded the object of Grayson's lust that it would be in her best interest if she forgot the whole incident. It also helped that Cain was able to convince her that the right amount of money could heal most wounds. To soften the blow to her ego, Cain entered into an intimate relationship with the woman. It lasted a few months and ended amicably. There would be no further repercussions.

After passing the New York State Bar Exam, the two Yalies, one privileged and one not, forged a relationship that would benefit each of them. Cain realized Grayson's potential early on and decided to ride the political wave while clearing the way for a presidential bid. Grayson had deep pockets and Cain had access to whatever resources were necessary to make it appear those situations never happened.

With Grayson's presidential campaign underway, Cain spent most of his time maintaining old business, assuring nothing from the senator's past reared its ugly head. All was going well until that damned reporter brought up Sheila Rand. Although Cain could handle the rumors that would fly, it was one more thing on his already long list. He had a more urgent concern.

Cain had anticipated Janet Maxwell's interference when her family perished in an accident, as he could no longer use them to deter her from dredging up the past. Seventeen years before, Cain had convinced Maxwell to give her child up for adoption. He devised what he thought was a clever way to keep her in line. For fifteen years, he'd provided information and photos of her daughter. It seemed to work. Once she married and had another child, she appeared satisfied with his progressively vague reports and, at times, disinterested in the girl.

As Grayson's political path took a definite shape, Cain told Maxwell he'd lost contact with the girl and her adoptive parents. He didn't want her to believe she had a means to threaten him or Grayson. For further insurance, Cain recently hired retired North Carolina police officer Ronald Glick to observe her routine and report anything out of the ordinary.

He first met Ronnie Glick at the last national convention held in Charlotte, North Carolina. The federal government had provided a hundred million in security grants for that year's conventions. When Charlotte expanded hiring to surrounding jurisdictions, Glick made the list of those sent from the Asheville Police Department.

Assigned to the Dunhill Hotel, where some members of Congress stayed, Glick was there to greet a stream of politicians, including Senator Todd Grayson and his personal counsel, Douglas Cain. A man of average height with a slight frame, Glick wore his uniform well—jacket and slacks cleaned, pressed, and fitted, along with spit-shined shoes. Standing outside the hotel entrance, he exuded efficacy.

The impression of efficiency and usefulness is what drew Cain to the North Carolina officer. He approached Glick late one evening after the day's events. They chatted about Glick's career, the fast pace of New York City and the Charlotte Hornets. Glick told Cain he had never married, was retiring at the end of the year, and would probably go stir-crazy. It was then Cain thought to add Glick to his payroll as a private investigator. He needed some new blood, someone willing to come to New York for a year or two, someone with no ties and available at any time.

His caution had paid off when Glick informed him that Maxwell hailed a cab and rode it to a Gramercy Park brownstone. P.I. Lucas Holt lived there. He knew Holt by his reputation and from his inquiry into the death of Sheila Rand. *What does Janet think she's doing?*

Lucas Holt's digging into the call girl's murder had been as aggravating as an invasive plant in the garden. He'd stopped when his daughter Marnie was abducted. *He brought it on himself.* After the kidnapping, talk of the Rand murder all but disappeared.

Cain swept aside a stack of files to clear the middle of his desk. He singled out an undersized gold key from a ring in his pocket and slid it into the lock of a concealed drawer. About to open it, he paused, pushed out of his chair, and strode to the door to secure it. His secretary would be in any moment, and he needed complete privacy.

He pulled the drawer open, removed a file, and spread the contents on the desktop. Focusing on one photo of the fifteen-year-old girl, he picked it up for a closer view. Cain studied her face and frowned. *She looks too much like her father.*

Checking his watch, he opened a burl wood cabinet and poured himself a drink. He gathered the papers and slid the picture in the folder. Cain wasn't sure why he kept the file, except that what it contained marked his transition from company lawyer to personal henchman.

Chapter 5

Leaving his air-conditioned law office at 666 Fifth Avenue, Cain's mind raced. *I need to be persuasive.*

Stepping outside the building was like entering a sauna wearing a fur coat. Cain loosened his tie. A Town Car waited to take him home. The driver leaned against the hood, talking on his cell phone. He ended the call as soon as he saw his boss and hurried to open the car door. Cain waved to him.

"I have to meet a client at her apartment before I call it a day, Jimmy. But I'll walk. It's not too far." *And I need more time to prepare.* "You go on home, and I'll get a cab when I'm done."

Jimmy removed his cap, wiping the sweat from his forehead. His brow knitted in confusion, and he looked around as if he could see the thick, muggy air that surrounded them.

"Heat's not too bad, I guess. Are you sure, Mr. Cain?"

"Yes, I'll see you in the morning."

"Okay, sir, have a good night." Jimmy rounded

the front of the car, tugging at the collar of his shirt, which stuck to his back under the wool-blend blazer he wore. He slipped into the driver's seat and pulled away.

Cain watched as Jimmy jerked the limo into traffic and weaved his way downtown. Once the car was out of sight, Cain turned and strolled north along Fifth Avenue. He wasn't in a particular hurry. He didn't actually have an appointment, but he intended to see a client, of sorts, whether she wanted to see him or not.

Twenty minutes later, Cain entered a Park Avenue apartment building and announced himself at the desk. The concierge made a phone call and when done, pointed to the elevators. Cain rode to the top floor. The lift opened directly into the apartment. A woman, dressed in a casual linen shift and sandals greeted him.

"Hello, Douglas. To what do I owe this pleasure?" She gave him a smile that did not reach her eyes.

"Hello, Janet. I hear you've been busy."

Janet Maxwell led Cain the length of the foyer, along a herringbone wood floor, to a bright living room, which overlooked Park Avenue. She sat on a tan, modern-style velvet sofa with a tufted back and pointed to the chair across from her.

"Sit down, Douglas."

As Cain settled into the seat, he scanned the eclectic room. Contemporary furniture of all materials mixed with a few antiques showcased an array of pottery, sculptures, and sterling framed photos. Large canvases of modern art covered the walls. He stared at one piece on the opposite wall from where he sat. Its black and white spiral had a hypnotic effect. It was an odd assortment, but Cain knew its value and marveled at how far Janet Maxwell had come in life since her relationship with Grayson.

"Nice apartment, Janet."

"Can I get you a drink?" She rose from the sofa and crossed the room to where a decanter of port and some glasses stood on a tray. "I'm having one."

"No, thanks." Cain adjusted himself in his seat and looked Janet in the eye when she sat down again.

"What are you doing, Janet?"

She relaxed against an animal print pillow and crossed her legs.

"Right now, I'm talking to you. It's so nice of you to visit. I've been lonely since…well, you know, since…" The words caught in her throat, and instead of continuing, she gulped her wine.

Cain watched her and wondered if it was an act. He knew Janet Maxwell as well as anyone could and didn't doubt she loved her husband and son. He also didn't doubt she could push her grief aside to focus on whatever she had set her mind on. At this time, Cain knew it was to locate her daughter. But he had to ask—straight out. There was no other way with her.

"Janet, did you hire Lucas Holt to find your daughter?"

For a split second, her eyes widened with alarm and then narrowed to a questioning squint. "Who's Lucas Holt? I don't know what you're talking about."

Cain eased out the breath he held and inhaled again. This was going to be harder than he thought.

"Don't play games with me, Janet. You were seen at Holt's brownstone and again at McAllister's. What do you think you're doing?"

"I don't know what anyone thought they saw, but I'm a free person and can go anywhere I like and see anyone I want—and I don't have to report to you."

"Janet, you made a deal a long time ago and were compensated. I've kept my end of the bargain by keeping you informed of your daughter for as long as I was able."

"It's been two years, Douglas, two years since you've given me any news of her. But that aside, I still don't know what you're implying."

"I'm not implying anything. I'm asking you outright. Are you trying to find your daughter? And if you've put such a thing in motion, you must stop it now."

"Again, I don't have the vaguest idea what you're talking about. But if I did decide to locate my child, it's no longer your concern."

"It will always be my concern. Anything that affects the life of Todd Grayson is my concern." Cain knew the second he finished speaking, it was the wrong thing to say.

Janet uncrossed her legs and leaned forward, her face tight with anger.

"Of course, it's all about Todd. That son of a bitch didn't give me a second glance once I told him I was carrying his child. He threw me away like a rag, and you used me to clean up his mess. I was young and foolish then, but I'm not anymore. I don't care about Todd or what happens to him. Leave me alone, Douglas."

She rose, set her glass down, and walked back through the foyer to the elevator. Cain had no choice but to follow.

"Janet, you're making a mistake. You need to be very careful."

Her head snapped up. She glared at him. "Are you threatening me, Douglas?"

Cain did not answer, but met her eyes stare for stare.

"You have nothing left to threaten me with. Everything I have is gone."

"There is the girl."

She raised an eyebrow. "And how will you use her against me if you don't know where she is?"

Cain's teeth clenched. His hands balled into fists. He wanted to punch this woman.

"Be careful, Janet. Remember, I know everything there is to know about you." He turned to press the elevator button. She grabbed his arm.

"No, Douglas, you be careful. I'm not a fool. I've taken precautions. If anything happens to me, you won't be able to save Todd Grayson or yourself."

CHAPTER 6

Three days after my meeting with Janet Maxwell at McAllister's, I stood on Gold Brook Covered Bridge, also known as Emily's Bridge, in Stowe, Vermont.

Local legend has it the bridge is haunted. A high school paper written in the late 1970s fueled the story of unrequited love and a young woman, Emily, who hanged herself on the bridge.

The three teens in the picture looked anything but suicidal. Janet Maxwell's daughter, who inherited her mother's blonde hair and upturned nose, posed with her friends, their arms slung over each other's shoulders, and they had wide grins on their faces.

Janet Maxwell hadn't received any updates about her daughter in two years. The meetings with the lawyer were in person, where he gave her a verbal report and handed her a photo. The only viable clue placing the girl in Stowe was the photo of the covered bridge. Janet Maxwell had thrown me a few fun facts about her daughter; one was her favorite movie was *Sound of Music*. She also thought the adoptive father's job was seasonal. That might not sound like much in the clue department. There are dozens of covered bridges and a seasonal job could be anything from tax accountant to pool cleaner. However, members of the famed von Trapp family own and operate one of the resorts in the area. It was worth a shot.

During my marriage, my ex-wife Susan and I toured New England and crossed more wooden bridges than I'd have liked. Using personal knowledge and an internet search, I had narrowed it down to three in the Stowe area. Emily's Bridge was the last one on my list. I parked the car on the side of the road a few yards from the entrance and got out.

Vermont is beautiful in any season. A summer shower had cut through the humidity and left the fresh scent of fragrant wildflowers and wet tree bark. I filled my lungs with clean country air.

I walked toward the structure, which resembled a barn set down in the middle of the road, dingy, damp, and gray—the color of tombstones. The bridge in the photo and the one in front of me were the same. A sudden cool breeze whipped through the tunnel opening. I shivered, though I wasn't cold. For a moment, I was rooted to where I stood. I imagined a distraught Emily, weeping into her hands as she prepared to end her life. I understood how helplessness could lead to hopelessness. Even though I hadn't found Marnie, I remained optimistic. To be hopeful is to survive.

Not a day goes by when I don't think of my

daughter. Always alive in my heart and mind, I pictured Marnie as her mother looked when she was a young woman. Tall and lean, with Susan's pert nose that crinkled when she smiled, not the aquiline one I inherited from my German ancestors. Marnie was born with deep blue eyes. Within six months, they had turned hazel. Susan bet me they'd be brown like hers by the time Marnie was a year old. I would have gladly lost that bet to have our daughter home.

Tires grinding into gravel interrupted my dismal thoughts. I turned to leave. My years as a police detective and private investigator instilled in me a habit of observation. Two cars parked nearby. A young couple sat inside a late-model blue compact. The other was a black Crown Victoria. The tinted windows obscured the passengers. I guessed they were waiting for sunset, when the moon rose to bask the bridge in an ethereal glow and set the scene for ghost watching. I didn't hang around, as I was looking for a young woman who was alive—at least I hoped she was.

I crossed the bridge, heading west on Gold Brook Road then north on Waterbury. Driving through the town of Stowe, I arrived at The Mountain Trail Inn. Susan and I had stayed in the expansive white house with wrap-around porches during our fall foliage visit. I wasn't feeling especially nostalgic, but it didn't occur to me to stay anywhere else.

My ex-wife and I had met while skiing in the Adirondacks. I was visiting my parents for a long weekend, and she was with a group of friends.

Susan stood out among the rest. I prefer brunettes or redheads to blondes, and Susan's rich chestnut color was an immediate attraction. Not only did I think she was beautiful, she exuded a serenity that counterbalanced my restless nature, and we both love the outdoors.

The interior of the inn had gone through a renovation since I was there sixteen years before. My room was on the first floor, furnished with two four-poster queen beds, a sitting area, and bath. The old air conditioner rattled and hummed, apparently not part of the redo. The sound grated on my nerves. The rain and darkness brought the temperature outside down to a comfortable, cool seventy degrees. I shut off the offending racket and raised the window a few inches. I peered through the glass and could see my Rover. The lot was dark except for one or two porch lights from separate inn accommodations across the way. My stomach growled, and I checked the time. It was after nine. Too late to eat a heavy meal.

The aroma of steak, seared over mesquite on a wood-burning grill, wafted in from a nearby restaurant. I almost changed my mind about skipping dinner. Instead, I removed the photo of the teens from my shirt pocket, leaned it against the cut-crystal bedside lamp, and dropped onto the nearest bed. I dozed to the sound of intermittent splashes as tires sloshed through puddles on the main road.

***

The hard click of a car door shutting jerked me

awake. I moved off the bed to stand behind the open curtain and peeked outside. The porch lights were off, but I could see another car had pulled up next to mine. I was about to return to bed thinking it was a latecomer to the inn when the movement of a small light caught my attention.

Someone was looking into my SUV, directing the light in each window. I wanted to shout at him to stay the hell away, but something about the car was familiar. I realized it was the Crown Victoria parked at the bridge—the one with the tinted windows.

The figure, medium height and thin as a rail, wore dark clothes and a black ball cap. The bill hid his face. I watched as he squatted and shone the light under the vehicle. He rose, shut off the flashlight, and leaned against his car.

I grabbed my duffel, took out a pair of night vision binoculars, and returned to the window. The figure had moved and wasn't where I could see him. I scanned the bumper for the license plate number. I wrote it down and continued to search for him in the lot.

Probably another guest, and I overreacted. I drove a Range Rover, equipped with all the bells and whistles, and people often stopped to admire it. It was midnight, though, in a darkened lot—not much to see and admire.

I tapped Ray Scully's number on my cellphone. He worked the night shift the last few months, so I figured he could use a wake-up call.

"Detective Scully."

"Hey, did I wake you?"

"Very funny, Holt. Haven't heard from you lately. How've you been?"

"Great. Hey, listen, I have a North Carolina plate I'd like you to run."

"Working on a case?"

"Yeah." I gave him the plate number. "Let me know when you ID the owner of the car. Thanks."

Before I could end the call, I heard Scully shout, "Hey, wait a minute."

"Yeah? What's up?" I knew an inquisition was about to start.

"I know you, Holt. Whenever you go mum on a case, I can bet you're digging on sacred ground, and somehow I'll be the one left holding the shovel."

"Relax, friend. It's just a missing person's case. Runaway teen."

"Yeah, sure. Okay, I'll get back to you about the plate."

"Thanks."

I hated lying to my old friend, but if I told him Grayson might be involved, I'd never hear the end of it.

Shutting the window, I glimpsed outside. Nothing had changed. I was about to call it a night again, when I heard something brush against my door and footsteps padding down the hall. I pressed my ear against it then jerked the door open and stepped into the empty hallway. The door across the hall swung open, and a man poked his head out.

"Oh, thought I heard someone at my door," he said.

"I thought the same. Seems we're both hearing things."

"Night," he said as he closed his door.

I didn't think I imagined it, but there was no sign of anyone. I ran back to the window—the Crown Victoria was still there.

Shrugging into a shirt to hide my holstered pistol, I left my room and hurried down the hall to the reception desk. A middle-aged woman with permed gray hair stood behind the desk. She was on the phone. When she saw me, she put up a finger for me to wait. Impatient, I was going to return to my room when she hung up.

"Can I help you?"

"Yes, I thought someone knocked on my door. A friend of mine said he might catch up with me here. Has anyone checked in, in the last half hour?"

"No, I'm sorry, no check-ins since eight o'clock. What's your friend's name? If he shows up, I can let you know. What room are you in, Mr....?"

"Holt. Never mind, he probably got tied up. I'll call him tomorrow. Thank you. Have a good night."

"Good night, Mr. Holt."

Exhausted, annoyed, and feeling a little ridiculous, I turned to go back to my room.

I slid my keycard into the slot and pushed the door open. I froze. My senses kicked into high gear and my focus sharpened.

Without air conditioning to mask the room's odors, I smelled the woodsy, metallic scent of aftershave mixed with sweat. The window was wide open. I scanned the room for anything out of place and zeroed in on the nightstand.

The photo of the girls on the covered bridge was gone.

CHAPTER 7

I woke at sunrise to the buzzing alarm. My phone told me it was sixty-nine degrees on a partly cloudy day.

Looking at the bright side, the stolen photo confirmed I was on the right track and someone was nervous. Who knew about my search for Janet Maxwell's daughter? Either Mrs. Maxwell let it slip she hired a PI or someone kept tabs on her. I was betting on the latter.

I was not without luck as fortune smiles on the prepared. I had scanned the photo to my phone as backup. While not as clear as the original, it would serve the purpose.

After a full breakfast and two cups of coffee, I headed to the public library on River Street. I've found in small towns every little thing is big news and decided to sift through local newspapers for high school events. Two of the girls in the photo would have just graduated.

As I moved about town, I was on the lookout for the Crown Victoria or a walking tail. I parked on a side street and strolled to the white clapboard, Greek Revival building. The massive double decker porch beckoned you to sit down and read your favorite book from start to finish.

I was surprised to find the inside modern while maintaining the original look and feel. A large room with a tray ceiling was furnished with joined desks and lamps. I could see nooks with comfortable chairs and people reading newspapers.

The woman at the front desk wore a bright, flowery dress, granny glasses, and an inviting smile. "How can I help you today, sir?"

"Hi. I would like to look at local newspapers covering the last couple of years."

"Certainly. Go straight back through the Calvin Coolidge room, and make a right into Justin Morrill Hall. You should see current newspapers and magazines. Below each are shelves with editions going back two years."

The same architecture carried over to the next room. Individual desks stood in the middle of the space, and brown, faux leather club chairs lined the window walls. Shelves spanning the length of the opposite wall held newspapers and magazines.

The Stowe Daily focused on everything local— news, sports, the arts, and high school events. Several editions showed pictures of Vermonters at the high school theater, on the links, or enjoying the picturesque countryside. I hoped to find one of the three girls from the covered bridge photo and get a name.

Two hours later, I found a picture of seven students in a high school version of *Thoroughly*

Modern Millie. An oval-faced cast member, with arms in the air, matched a girl at the covered bridge. The caption only mentioned the name of the star: Caitlin Jennings. Crosschecking the phone book with a map of Stowe allowed me to eliminate three Jennings as too far from the high school, leaving one on Houston Farm Lane.

It was a five-minute drive to a weathered gray Cape Cod house with a red door and black shutters. As I pulled up, threatening dark clouds rolled in from the west. A heavyset woman opened the door, hurried to her car, and raised the windows.

"Hello!" I gave her my irresistible smile and sauntered up the driveway.

She eyed the front door. Her escape route was too far. "Yes?"

"Mrs. Jennings? My name is Lucas Holt. Could I have a moment of your time?" She gave me a look as if I were an insurance salesman. "I'm a private investigator." I showed her my P.I. license. Annoyance replaced dread. I guessed I was the lesser of two evils.

"Oh. What is this about?"

"I have a client who is searching for a young lady she hasn't seen in seventeen years." I wasn't able to tell her the whole truth. I showed her the picture on my phone. "Do you know any of these girls?"

When she didn't respond I added, "There's a sum of money involved for the girl."

"That's Barbara Hansen on the right. I don't know the other two girls. They look like they could be sisters, though."

She was right. Maxwell's daughter and one of the girls had the same golden hair, round face, and athletic build. Barbara Hansen, taller and heavier, had dark hair and a pronounced nose. Mrs. Jennings didn't know Janet Maxwell's daughter. I had hoped she would name all three girls.

"I wonder if your daughter, Caitlin, would mind looking at the picture." I flashed my winning smile again. How could she refuse?

She frowned. Did I have something in my teeth?

"Wait here," she said after a moment.

She entered the house and closed the door. I noticed Caitlin peeking through white lace curtains upstairs. While waiting, I glanced up and down the street. There were few places one could hide without being deemed suspicious by a neighbor. Every car, as far as I could see, was in a driveway.

The door opened. Mrs. Jennings and her daughter appeared, Caitlin's arms folded across her chest.

"Hi. Thanks so much for taking time to talk to me."

Caitlin was silent. Mom responded, "Sorry we took so long. Can we see the picture again?"

I handed my phone to Caitlin. She stared at the picture and her expression changed to a grimace. Finally, she looked up, pointed at the girl on the right.

"Barbara Hansen and I are friends. That's Karen Martin in the middle and Mary Wells on the left. I don't know them very well."

I had a name. Janet Maxwell's daughter was Karen Martin.

"Thank you. Do you know if these girls still live in this area?"

I sensed Caitlin's reluctance to speak. An interrogator's trick is to let the silence linger, and it would soon be filled. "Barbara does. I think Karen moved. I don't know where."

"Perhaps Barbara can help me locate Karen. Does she live nearby?"

"I'll ask her if she'll talk to you." Caitlin spun around, pulled out her cellphone, and walked a short distance.

I turned to Mrs. Jennings. "I think I may have intimidated Caitlin a bit."

"It's okay. I told her I saw your license and photo. You are who you say you are."

Caitlin returned. "Barbara lives five houses down on the opposite side of the street. The house is a white split level."

"Thanks again, to both of you." I started to walk back to the car when Caitlin spoke.

"You know…you're not the first person to show me that picture."

CHAPTER 8

"Someone else showed you this picture?" I held out the photo of the girls at the covered bridge.

"Yes."

"Where did this happen?"

"At our soccer game. I thought he was a parent until I noticed him walking around, showing something to a lot of people. Now I think it must have been the photograph."

Initially Caitlin was reluctant to speak. Then she became more willing and provided a key piece of information. I wanted to keep the flow going, so I used my engaging smile.

"Did your team win?" Her mom nodded from behind her.

"This isn't funny." Mrs. Jennings was getting ready to interject when I apologized.

"Okay. Sorry." *Kids, huh?* "Did he show you any identification?"

"He showed me a police badge, but I've seen police badges. This one looked fake."

Mr. Crown Vic was likely the person who stole

the picture from my hotel room.

"Can you remember his name?"

"No. I barely got a look at his ID."

"Last question, Caitlin. Can you describe the man?"

"He wasn't much taller than me and thin. His face was long, and he had a black mustache that curled down around his lips. He brushed his hair straight back. And he carried a black cap."

As I'd only seen him in the shadows, her description filled in some blanks.

"I thought he looked like a creep and didn't tell him anything," she added.

A break for the good guys.

Her face scrunched up, and she pointed her index finger at me. "And he smiled at me the same lame way you did."

***

Parked in one of the neighboring driveways, Ronnie Glick removed his cap and scratched his head. He sat slumped in the seat of his rented Jeep Cherokee. Caitlin Jennings' house was within sight. Lucas Holt had returned to his car after his conversation with the girl. Glick waited for Holt to drive off, intending to follow him. His cellphone rang.

"Glick here."

"It's Cain. What's going on? What's Holt up to?"

"He was talking to a teenager and her mother."

"So he's making progress. Remember why

you're there. You need to find out what he knows. What have you done to that end?"

"Well, last night I was able to get into his hotel room and remove a photo he had of three girls. Figured I could use it, and he wouldn't have anything to show around."

Glick could hear Cain's low audible breathing. He imagined a dragon breathing fire.

"Did you rent a car to replace your own?"

"I did, but not 'til this morning."

"I hope you were discreet."

"Yes sir, I'm pretty sure he didn't see me. I saw an opportunity and managed to draw him out of his room. It took less than a minute to get in and out."

"What photo?" Glick described it to Cain. "Yeah, I know the one. What did you do with it?"

"I used it to show around at the high school. No one would tell me anything. I'm tailing Holt. He spent a few hours in the library. Now, I'm sitting in a driveway a few houses down from where he is, waiting for him to pull away."

Glick could hear Cain's heavy drawn breath again. "Sir?"

"I wouldn't be surprised if Holt knows who you are already."

"I don't think so, Mr. Cain."

"Glick, you have no idea who you're dealing with. Never mind. It's my fault for not thinking this through. You're not there to investigate and call attention to yourself. I need to know where he goes. Tail him, but keep your distance. I'll call back in a few hours."

"Sure thing, sir." Glick barely said the words

before Cain ended the call.

Holt's SUV still sat in front of the Jennings' house. Ronnie Glick wiped his forehead, took a swig of his bottled water, and slouched back against the seat to wait.

***

I sat in the Rover, mesmerized by the steady stream of pelting rain on my windshield.

Turning on the wipers, I looked ahead and behind me. The black Crown Victoria was not in sight. I asked myself, if I were Mr. Crown Vic, what would I do? I'd follow Lucas Holt. I'd know Holt spotted my car and possibly my North Carolina license plate. I'd rent another ride.

I glanced in the side rearview mirror and spotted someone sitting in a white Jeep Cherokee parked in a driveway. The driver wasn't clearly visible. As I pulled away and rounded a curve, the Jeep backed out. I parked on the opposite side of the street near the house of Caitlin's friend Barbara. The Jeep followed and came to a near stop before accelerating away.

Running between raindrops up the walk, I approached a stained-glass door with two frosted side panels. Before I could ring the bell, the door opened. A plump, dark-haired girl came outside and smiled. We stood under a portico.

"Hi. I'm Barbara."

"Hi, Barbara, I'm Lucas Holt. Did Caitlin tell you about our conversation?"

"Just that you were looking for Karen Martin."

"Yes. I understand she moved away. Do you know where?"

"Not sure, I think Pennsylvania or maybe that's where she said she was going to college. She told me it was somewhere in the middle of nowhere. I know she was bummed to be moving again after making friends here."

"It's always tough to leave your friends. Did you know her parents?"

"Yes, they were very nice. Her mom was quiet, hardly left the house. I don't think she knew how to drive because we used to pick up Karen for school sometimes. Her dad worked at the Snow Drift Lodge as an instructor. I took a few lessons from him. He liked his job, and I wondered why they moved."

"Maybe another job opportunity."

Barbara shrugged.

"Do you know Mary Wells?"

"Yes. She was best friends with Karen. They were like sisters."

"Do you know where Mary Wells lives? Maybe she could tell me where Karen is."

"Yeah, she might. She lives on Cranbury Road. I think number forty-nine. I haven't seen her around since school ended."

I wrote down the address.

"You told Caitlin there was money involved. Did someone die and leave Karen money?"

"Something like that." I changed the subject following that white lie. "The photo I have is two years old. Do you have anything more recent?"

"I can check my Facebook photos. We used to be

friends but she closed her account. Wait here."

Barbara appeared eager to help. She came back in ten minutes with a picture.

"This photo is not clear," Barbara said, handing me a piece of copy paper.

The grainy photocopy showed Karen Martin as she sat on a large rock on the edge of a wooded area. Her knees touched her chest and she hugged her legs. Her matured features drew a striking resemblance to her mother. I could see a hint of the senator's contribution in her expression.

"You said she closed her Facebook account. I imagine you don't keep in touch any other way."

"No, not really. But people reactivate their accounts all the time."

"Barbara, thank you. You've been a big help. Here's my card. If Karen happens to reopen her account or you have anything else you can tell me, contact me any time. When I find Karen, I'll tell her how helpful you were."

The rain finally let up. I punched Mary Wells' address into my GPS. I was going to head over there when Ray Scully called. I noticed the time. It was late afternoon.

"Hey, buddy, did they take you off the night shift?"

"No, it's my day off. I'm on my sixth cup of coffee. My body is telling me I should be asleep, but my wife is saying otherwise. Her parents are coming for dinner. They're in town and want to see the kids. If my father-in-law starts describing his golf game to me, I'm in trouble. No amount of coffee will keep me awake for that."

"I still envy you, pal. You have something for me?"

"Yeah, that plate is registered to a retired North Carolina police officer named Ronald Glick. He retired almost two years ago. Last known address, eight twenty five Maple Leaf Avenue, Black Mountain, North Carolina."

"A police officer? The guy has balls. He climbed in my window and stole a photo of the missing girl."

"Where were *you* when he climbed through the window?"

I thought about how Glick was able to get me to leave my room.

"Never mind." I skirted around that line of questioning. "Thanks for the info. I'll be out of town for a couple of weeks, but when I get back you can buy me a beer."

"Buy *you* a beer? I'm still living on a detective's salary. The beer's on you."

"Okay, sure, I might even throw in a steak. It'll be a change from all the mac and cheese you're used to eating. Give my love to Regina and the kids."

"I will. Let me know if you need anything else."

"Yep, will do."

I really did envy Scully. As lucrative as my line of work is, the comforts it provides are only superficial. My former partner enjoys true luxury— the kind money can't buy.

***

The rain clouds moved further west, and I followed them on my way to Mary Wells' house. I turned off a main road to a lane that wound through a wooded incline. The blacktop was slippery and masses of towering red oaks and pine trees blocked out most of the natural light. I opened the window and inhaled the fresh pine scent.

A sudden clearing at the end of the road split into two driveways. I took the one on the right and pulled up to a large farmhouse, which backed up to acres of mowed lawn. There were no cars in the driveway. I climbed the porch steps, rang the bell, and knocked on the door. No one answered.

I turned to the railing and glanced out toward another house in the distance—the one at the end of the left driveway. A woman stood on her porch, peering at me. Since she appeared interested, I decided to alleviate her curiosity and mine.

Dressed for gardening in short-cropped pants, a long-sleeved blouse and huge straw hat, the Wells' neighbor greeted me with a nod as I pulled up her driveway.

"Good evening, ma'am, I'm Lucas Holt." I held out my card. She accepted it with her garden-gloved hand.

"Evening. You looking for the Wells?"

"Yes, but I see they're not home."

She gave me a tight-lipped, "No."

"Do you know if they'll be back tonight or tomorrow—I'm sorry what did you say your name was?"

She raised a penciled eyebrow. "I didn't, and I'm not going to give out any information about the comings and goings of my neighbors."

"Okay, well I'm looking for the Martins. I was told Mary Wells was a friend of their daughter's."

"I knew the Martins. They moved."

"Do you know where they moved to?"

"Nope."

"Oh. Okay. Thank you." I turned toward the Rover, thinking the only good thing about the lead was the drive up the mountain. Then the woman spoke.

"You could ask Kathryn Sullivan."

CHAPTER 9

"Who's Kathryn Sullivan?" I asked.

"She and her husband live in the Martin house now. She works at the library at the reference desk. It's open 'til seven tonight."

Stunned she volunteered that bit of information, I almost forgot to thank her.

"Appreciate it. Have a good evening."

She nodded, climbed the steps to her porch, and returned to her post. I could see her in my rearview mirror. She kept a steady watch as I drove down her drive and back onto the lane.

It was six fifteen, more than enough time to drive the few miles back to town and catch Mrs. Sullivan before the library closed.

I parked off the main road, headed to the library on foot. The same cheerful woman greeted me. This time I noticed the nameplate on her desk.

"Hi, Mrs. Crawford, is Kathryn Sullivan here today?"

"No, I'm sorry. Can I help you with something?"

"When will she return to work?"

"Not for a few days. She's on vacation."

"I'm told Mrs. Sullivan lives in the house that belonged to the Martins. Did you happen to know them?" I asked, handing her my card.

"A private investigator?" Mrs. Crawford lost her smile and scowled. "No, I don't believe I do. Perhaps you should wait for Kathryn to come back. I don't think I can help you."

I wasn't going to get any more from her. I thanked her and left.

***

The day had started out clear and sunny, but clouds took over as I made my way to the Snow Drift Lodge. I found it with relative ease even though my GPS, which I call Gypsy, sometimes has trouble calculating in mountainous areas, especially on rainy days. There was no sign of a white Cherokee or a black Crown Victoria on my tail.

The lodge, nestled between two mountains, consisted of a center building flanked by long annexes, three-stories high. The connecting wings formed two right angles enclosing an outdoor courtyard, which held a resort-style pool with a slide. I entered the four-story, marble-floored lobby. A contrasting, timbered ceiling soared to a center peak. Tall, thin birch trunks leaned against marble pillars. Multi-light chandeliers hung from the timbers. Sofas and chairs upholstered in the colors of fall foliage created several cozy seating areas.

I presented my ID at the reception desk and asked for the manager. A few minutes later, a Mr.

Ingram introduced himself and led me to one of the seating areas.

"How can I help you, Mr. Holt?"

"I'm trying to locate a young woman who is the recipient of a large inheritance, and I understand her father worked for you." I had begun to feel comfortable with the lie. "His name is Daniel Martin."

"Oh, yes, Daniel was a ski instructor here for many years. He and his family moved to Pennsylvania a year ago. I believe he said his daughter might attend college there, so they wanted to be close to her. I imagine he works at one of the ski resorts."

"You don't happen to remember if any of them called you for a reference?"

"Well, now that you mention it, someone did call, but I don't remember which resort. I'm afraid I didn't make note of it."

"Did he leave a forwarding address? And perhaps you could give me his prior address here in Stowe."

"Let me check his employment file. One moment, please."

With Mr. Ingram on his way to his office, I stood and walked toward one of the tall picture windows and scanned the outside view. I thought it must be gorgeous in winter during a light snowfall. About to go back to my seat, I noticed a man in black jeans and t-shirt cross the lobby from the bank of elevators. He strode to the entrance, slipped on sunglasses and a black ball cap.

It had to be Glick.

I moved closer to the entrance, hoping he wouldn't turn around. He exited and I could see through the large glass as he entered the parking lot. He stopped short when he saw my Rover, which I had parked out front. He glanced around and back at the hotel. I stepped behind one of the marble pillars and watched him go a few rows to another area of the lot and get into a Cherokee.

The resort manager returned and, unfortunately, the Martins had not left a forwarding address. He did provide me with their Stowe address. I wondered about Mr. Glick's presence in the hotel.

"Mr. Ingram, I thought I saw an associate of mine leave the hotel. Would you mind checking to see if he is registered here? His name is Ronald Glick."

Mr. Ingram sighed and turned toward the reception desk. I followed.

Glick was indeed a guest. I thanked Mr. Ingram and checked to see if the Cherokee was still there. It was. Mr. Glick was waiting to pick up my tail again. I exited through the back of the hotel. Passing the pool, I walked around the right wing of the resort—in the opposite direction from where Glick sat in his car.

I took a long stroll around the resort and found what I was looking for—the black Crown Victoria with North Carolina plates. I needed to lose this guy. The lot was void of people, the security guard was on a break, and Mr. Glick could not see me from where he parked. I took out my switchblade—one of those things a prepared PI never leaves home without—and slashed three of the four tires on

Glick's car.

I wasn't done with Glick and thought a little intimidation was warranted. The jeep was in a corner spot in one of the few tree-shaded areas of the lot. Walking along the property's fence, I crept up to the Cherokee from behind. Glick, apparently too intent on watching my Rover to notice my arrival, jumped when I jerked the car door open. Using both hands, I yanked him out by the shirt collar and pressed his back against the Cherokee.

"I'll do the talking," I told him.

My face was so close to his, I could see flecks of dandruff in his mustache. "I know who you are, Glick. I don't want to hurt you, so this is just a warning. Get off my back. Tell whoever hired you that you've been made. On the other hand, maybe I can do that for you. Empty your pockets. Slow with no sudden moves."

Glick's eyes narrowed. I could tell he was no longer shocked and frightened but pissed. Glaring at me, he produced his wallet, cell, and car keys. I pocketed the phone and keys.

In a surprise move, he landed a hook to the side of my head. Stepping back, I blocked another hook and threw a flurry of jabs. Glick's legs began to weaken, and I thought he would pass out. I didn't intend to hurt him, just send him home with his tail between his legs. By punching me, he'd taken a step up in class. I wanted him to remember the moment. I held Glick up, pushed him into the back seat, and threw his wallet on the floor. I searched under the seats and the glove compartment for a weapon. There wasn't one. I did find the photo he stole from my room. I left Glick in the car in a half-dazed state and returned to my Rover. I drove away and decided not to go back to my hotel to check out. If Glick was foolish enough to continue following me, he could assume I was still in Stowe.

A half a mile away, I pulled over and entered the Martins' prior address into Gypsy. I drove to the house where Kathryn Sullivan now lived. There were no cars in the driveway and no one answered the doorbell. I called information for the Sullivan's phone number and luckily, it was listed. I left a message on the machine and my card with a note in the mailbox. Regardless what the Sullivans might tell me, I had a lead. The Martins were in Pennsylvania.

Before leaving Stowe, I had one more thing to do. Checking the calls on Glick's phone, I hit send for the last number. There was an immediate answer. The man's voice sounded strained and angry.

"Glick, I told you I'd call you in a few hours. What do you want?"

"This is not Glick."

"What? Where is he? What's happened to him?"

"I'm sorry. Mr. Glick is unavailable."

The man shouted, "Who the hell is this? How'd you get this phone?"

"It was easier than I imagined. I don't know who you are, but I have an idea who you work for, and I have some advice for both of you. Call off Glick. You'll have to do a lot more than attach him to my tail to keep me from doing my job."

I disconnected the call and left Stowe as the

clouds cleared and the sun, a giant red ball, sank behind the mountains.

CHAPTER 10

Glick held a towel packed with ice on his jaw as he paced his hotel room and planned what to do next.

After coming out of his Holt-induced stupor, he assessed the damage. He had no phone and no keys for the Jeep. But he could use the Crown Victoria. He'd rushed to his room to get the keys and back to the parking lot, stunned to find it wasn't drivable. He had spent the better part of the afternoon arranging to have his car towed for repair.

The dumb-as-dirt security guard couldn't imagine how someone could slash a car's tires while he was on duty. Never mind that he parked on the other side of the resort to have a smoke. The guard had looked at the Crown Victoria, scratched his chin, and asked, "How come only three tires are slashed?"

Idiot. But Glick had wondered too. He couldn't think of a good reason other than leaving one tire intact made the deed more noticeable.

Glick sought out the hotel manager.

"Oh, yes, Mr. Glick, did your friend catch up with you?"

Glick's brows furrowed. "Friend?"

"Actually, he said he was an associate of yours—Lucas Holt. He saw you leave the hotel earlier and inquired if you were a guest here. He used to be in law enforcement too, so I didn't see a problem."

Glick wasn't pleased the manager told Holt anything but knew you could catch more flies with honey than with vinegar.

"No, no problem at all. As a matter of fact, I did see him in the parking lot."

It didn't take long for Mr. Ingram to tell Glick what he told Lucas Holt, which wasn't much except the general whereabouts of the Martins. He believed they moved to Pennsylvania.

***

The car rental agency brought Glick another set of keys, for which he had to pay dearly. It was evening when he called Douglas Cain from a new burner phone to give him an edited version of what had happened.

"I know what happened," Cain said. "You fucked up and got too close." Glick knew the lawyer was not happy to hear Holt had a good lead on the location of the girl and a head start over him. Cain, whose voice sounded strained to Glick, told him to forget about Holt and return to New York.

"But, Mr. Cain, I'm sure I can pick up his tail again."

"No, it's been hours."

"I called his hotel, he's not checked out. I—"

"Just come back to New York."

"Sir, I think you're making a mistake. If—"

"Glick! Holt's probably halfway to Broome by now! It's over. Get back here ASAP."

"Yes, sir. I understand. I'll be back as soon as my tires are replaced."

"Forget the car. Have it flat-bedded back here. Drive back in the rental."

Glick needed to buy more time. "Okay, but it's too late to arrange today," he lied. "I'll do it first thing in the morning and be on my way after that."

"Fine. I need you to keep an eye on Janet Maxwell again."

Glick hung up. *So Cain hasn't been straight with me. He's known where the girl is the whole time.*

Ronnie Glick decided, since Holt made him look like a buffoon, he'd retaliate—a plan was already forming in his mind. *I'm tired of babysitting Ms. Posh.* He was trained for better than that. He would show Cain his real value.

Ah, screw Cain.

He wondered how long it would take Cain to realize he'd blurted out the name of the Pennsylvania town. He was now one giant step ahead of Holt. The head start would give him time to plan a diversion for Holt with the added bonus of some payback.

It was midnight when Glick, traveling south on NY-17, merged the rented Cherokee onto I-287 and entered New Jersey on his way toward Broome, Pennsylvania.

***

Glick reached Broome at midmorning and drove around to get a feel for the town. Well-kept buildings, clean streets, and a profusion of flowers in hanging pots reminded Glick of villages in the south.

A few residents walked along the main street, buying a newspaper or fresh baked goods from the bakery. An older couple entered a church for weekday services as the bells pealed. Glick felt he'd stepped onto a set of a fifties family sitcom. He stopped in a coffee shop, sat at the counter, and ordered the breakfast special.

An elderly man, who sat a seat away, looked at Glick with cataract-laden blue eyes. He rubbed his veined nose with the back of his hand and scratched his chin through four days' worth of growth. He drank coffee, but he smelled like whiskey. The man nodded a hello.

Glick ignored him and dug into his eggs.

Not deterred, the man spoke, "New to town, are ya?"

His mouth full of home fries, Glick nodded.

"That your Cherokee out there? Vermont plates on it. That where you're from?"

Glick's eyes shifted toward the man. "Just passing through."

"Through to where?"

Unprepared for the man's questions, he squirmed in his seat and shoved some eggs into his mouth. Glick searched his brain. *What's the nearest big city?* The man sat staring, waiting for an answer.

Pittsburgh! "Pittsburgh. Yeah, that's where I'm going, Pittsburgh."

"You sound southern. What do ya do in Pittsburgh?"

Ronnie Glick put down his fork, wiped his mouth with a napkin, and asked for the check.

"I'm going to visit a friend," he said in a clipped tone.

The man turned to face Glick.

"I got friends in Pittsburgh. What's your friend's name?"

What the hell? Glick had enough. He threw the cost of the meal plus two dollars on the counter, grabbed his black cap and left.

The plan forming in Ronnie Glick's head wouldn't work in Broome. If the old man were any indication of the type of people in the small town, he'd never be able to pull it off. He needed to go to another town—some place where people don't care who you are or where you're from—only how much you'll pay for a job—any job. He thought he knew just the place.

CHAPTER 11

Grabbing my cup of coffee, I settled into the overstuffed cushion of a wrought-iron lounge chair on my patio.

The nineteenth-century brownstone I purchased five years ago, nestled in the enclave of Gramercy Park, is my oasis. Clematis, trumpet vine, and climbing hydrangea cover the high concrete walls that enclose my personal paradise. I can identify these perennial vines as my gardener, Pasquale, insists I know by name the beauty that surrounds me. It's hard to believe I could find serenity in one of the busiest cities in the world—it's hard to believe I could find serenity at all.

Hours in the garden with my laptop, doing internet searches of ski resorts where Daniel Martin might seek employment, yielded a couple of possibilities. Remembering Barbara Hansen's remark about the Martins moving to the middle of nowhere, I discounted the Poconos and other large ski areas. I had a fleeting thought doing so might be a mistake as teenagers tend to have their own view of *nowhere*.

Before I set out on another wild goose chase, I called Scully to ask him to check the DMV for Daniel Martin's driver's license. Since moving to another state, he might have had a new one. He agreed to check, but before obliging me, he wanted a few particulars about the case.

"Lucas, anything more I can do besides the DMV? You say this is about a runaway teen. Who is Daniel Martin? Her father?"

"Yeah, well, not exactly a runaway—more like a missing person. In fact, run the name Karen Martin too. She's old enough to drive."

"Who's looking for the teen? The mother?"

"Yes."

"Parents are divorced, I guess."

"No."

"Okay, now I'm getting one-word answers. I have an uneasy feeling, Holt. You're usually a little more giving. Ease my mind…tell me who the mother is."

"You know that information is confidential."

"It's not if you want my help."

"Sorry, Scully. No can do. Listen, I have to go. I appreciate anything you can find out."

"Yeah, later."

I missed working cases with Scully. We grew up in different environs. I lived in a small town in the Adirondacks until I joined the Army Rangers. Scully was Brooklyn-born into a family of cops. We made a good team; we both had a profound respect for the law. But life happens, and I realized in some instances working on the fringe got better results.

The last case we worked together was the Bowery call girl murder.

After cleaning up a few dirty dishes, I entered my second-floor office and scanned the room. A box of files pertaining to the unsolved case remained tucked in a corner, for years, in whichever room I used as an office, wherever I called home. A constant reminder of what led me to become who I am.

Although close by, I hadn't opened the file for some time. I dusted off the box and moved it to the floor next to my desk. Janet Maxwell's admission that she knew about Grayson's relationship with the girl was new evidence in the case. I should have told Scully.

Since I needed to hear from Scully before moving forward, I closed the Maxwell file and turned my attention to the murder of Sheila Rand.

Rand, twenty-six years old, receptionist by day, call girl by night, had resided in one of the more seedy buildings in the Bowery section of New York. The rundown walkup was a few blocks from the high-priced, steel-and-glass building in which Grayson lived.

When Sheila didn't show up for work for two days, and phone calls to her apartment were unanswered, the superintendent was called to let the police inside. Scully and I arrived at the secured scene on a Wednesday morning. The familiar smell of putrefaction told us the victim had been dead a few days. It was later determined she died on the previous Saturday.

Rand's partially clothed body lay on the floor

next to her bed. A glance at the numerous wounds and blood splatter indicated a stabbing. The assailant had inflicted several shallow stabs and one deep penetrating wound in the stomach, where he thrust the weapon in and up toward the heart. The medical examiner ruled it cause of death. Other lacerations on Rand's arms and hands showed she had put up a fight. The autopsy revealed drugs and alcohol in her system. In her condition, Rand wouldn't have been able to sustain much of a defense against her attacker.

There was no evidence of sexual assault or consensual sex. Her clothes, removed in a haphazard way, were probably ripped off in the struggle. In addition to the stab wounds, an earring had been ripped from her lobe and clumps of her hair pulled out.

The most damning piece of evidence was her diary in which she recorded an appointment with TG on Saturday at 10:00 p.m. That and the corroboration of an eyewitness, who said he saw the senator enter the apartment building, led us to Todd Grayson.

I reread the eyewitness statement from Henry Williams, the resident of a nearby building, who was later discredited as being unreliable due to his addiction to heroin. Grayson's lawyers insisted someone paid Williams to give false evidence. He had an expensive habit to support. As I pulled out photos of the crime scene, my phone rang. It was Scully.

"That was fast," I said.

"Yeah, fast and uninformative. Both Daniel and

Karen Martin have Vermont driver's licenses that don't expire for years."

"I was afraid of that. I didn't ask this before because I didn't have a name, but what about his tax returns? If he was working the last year or two, he would have filed a return."

"Lucas, checking the DMV is one thing, but I have to have a good reason to pull tax records. Remember, you don't work for law enforcement, and I'm not working this case."

I thought about mentioning Janet Maxwell's admission. But that would have opened a whole new can of worms, and I needed to stay focused on finding her daughter. I knew I'd find the Martins— it would just take longer without Scully's help.

"Okay, Ray, thanks again."

"Anytime. Hey, I look forward to that beer."

I spent the rest of the afternoon calling ski resorts in Pennsylvania without any success. Maybe Martin no longer worked as a ski instructor. If that was the case and I had nowhere to go, I would have to tell Scully about Maxwell and Sheila Rand. Even then, there was no connection to Maxwell's daughter. But it might be incentive for Scully to check into Martin's tax returns.

Around six o'clock I walked down to McAllister's for a burger and brew. I didn't stay long. For some reason, since my meeting with Janet Maxwell, the place was not the same haven it had been. I returned home angry and frustrated and had worked up a sweat from the brisk walk through the humid streets of the city.

My bedroom and bath are on the third floor. I

poured two fingers of Johnny Walker and headed for the shower. Naked, I glanced at myself in the full-length mirror, noticing old scars from my days in the Army and a fading bruise from a recent encounter in the Catskills. Superficial wounds. They fade. They're forgotten. I downed my scotch, fortification for the wounds that never heal. I was about to hit the steam when my phone rang.

"This is Holt."

"Mr. Holt, this is Bob Ingram, manager at the Snow Drift Lodge."

"Yes, Mr. Ingram, how are you?"

"I'm fine. I received a strange message, and I thought you'd be interested. I have to tell you the coincidence is quite disturbing."

"Something to do with the case I'm working on?"

"Yes."

"Who left you a message?"

"Daniel Martin."

CHAPTER 12

I don't believe in coincidence or fate.

The telephone message from Daniel Martin given to a reception desk clerk at the Snow Drift Lodge was suspect. I had my suspicions about who was behind it. Not having any other leads, I told Ingram I would talk to Mr. Martin.

Eager to call the number Bob Ingram provided, I cut short the long, soothing steam shower I had planned. I toweled off, slipped on some shorts and a tee, and picked up my cell.

I liked the good old days when a phone number told you something. You could match an exchange with a particular location. With cellphones, especially the prepaid variety, it's almost impossible to trace a call. Traditional cellphone carriers lease or sell blocks of numbers to distributors. The user has usually tossed the phone by the time you find out there is no information on file anyway.

It was late, but I tried the number. No answer and no voice mail. After ten rings, the call disconnected.

* * *

The next morning after downing a cup of strong Kona coffee and a couple of fried eggs, I retreated to my office. My workspace and haven—the pride and joy of a meticulous renovation—encompasses the rear half of the second and third floors of the brownstone. The centerpiece of the lower-floor office is a custom-made, African ribbon mahogany desk with brass handles. Bookcases and panels made from a blend of rich woods line two opposite walls. Floor to ceiling windows on both sides of a Tudor-style stone fireplace allow enough light to keep the space from feeling like a dungeon. Drapes on wooden rods and a few club chairs upholstered in a Tartan plaid provide a subdued tone.

Original art pieces, acquired over the years, cover all available wall space. I love the cornucopia of New York artists and prefer to choose my art from the unfiltered array of works found at the city's street fairs.

Ten feet above and around the perimeter of the room is a five-foot-wide gallery, edged by a wood and iron railing. A spiral staircase leads to more book-filled shelves and access to the master bedroom. You might not associate an office with a retreat, but work is what I live for and what has kept me sane for the past fifteen years.

Before I delved into the pile on the desk, I again tried the number Ingram gave me. Three rings and someone answered, "Hello?"

"Hello. I'm looking for Daniel Martin."

"Yes? Who is this?"

"Is this Daniel Martin?"

"That depends. Who are you?"

I hate telephone games.

"I'm Lucas Holt, Mr. Martin. Bob Ingram gave me your number. You left him a message."

"I did. I need a reference."

I didn't know what part of the country Daniel Martin was from, but I noticed a soft twang when he spoke. Southern, I determined—like Carolina southern. I couldn't be sure and had to be careful not to scare the man, if he was Martin. I gave him the story that was starting to feel more and more like the truth.

"I'd like to talk to you about your daughter. I'm a private investigator and have been hired to find Karen Martin regarding some money that has been left to her. "

"An inheritance? Really?"

I detected slight amusement in the voice, where there should have been curiosity. That made me wary.

"Yes. I'd like to discuss the details with you, as her guardian."

"Sure, Mr. Holt. Perhaps you'd like to do that in person."

"Yes. I'd also like to meet your daughter, if possible."

"I'm not able to travel to you," he said, ignoring my request to meet Karen. "Where did you say you were calling from?"

"I'm on the road. I can come to you."

"Okay, but I'd prefer to meet you outside my home. I don't know you and feel more comfortable in a public place. Is a neighborhood bar and grill okay with you?"

"Sure. When and where?"

"Well, how about tomorrow evening at 8:00 p.m. at the Gunslinger's Saloon in Smoulder, Pennsylvania?"

It sounded like a joke, and I almost laughed out loud at the name of the bar.

"Sounds great. See you then, Mr. Martin."

We disconnected, and I sat a few minutes to rerun the conversation in my mind. There was no way to verify whom I spoke with since Ingram hadn't spoken to Martin first to confirm it was him. I had to admit that was a mistake. But after mulling it over, if someone were posing as Martin, he most likely wouldn't have answered Ingram's return call. Convinced the call was meant for me, I'd prepare accordingly.

Gunslinger's Saloon. I'd definitely pack some heat—maybe a white hat wouldn't hurt.

***

Later that day I took some time to organize the files and loose papers strewn all over my desk. I never liked to leave my office untidy. First, because I am a bit of a neat freak, and second, the nature of my work is confidential. I scan most case information to my computer, which I back up on a separate hard drive and memory stick and shred the hard copy.

The Rand files were an exception. I always had a tactile need when it came to that case. It represented a turning point in my life—I needed to engage all the senses. The folder of crime scene photos and written reports protruded out of the box. I removed it to take with me and closed the carton. Climbing the staircase to the gallery with the Rand files, I entered my bedroom and locked them in a large safe in the back of my closet.

As I stuffed a suitcase with a week's worth of clothes and necessities, my cellphone rang.

"Lucas Holt."

"Mr. Holt, this is Janet Maxwell. I know it's only been a couple of days, but do you have anything to tell me?"

"So far, my search is leading me to Pennsylvania."

"Pennsylvania? Nothing more specific?"

Since I was sure Karen Martin wasn't in Smoulder, and I like my clients to feel I'm making progress, I decided to be more specific. "I'm heading to a town called Smoulder to meet someone who may be able to tell me where your daughter is. By the way, it appears there's a tail on me. Do you happen to know who would do that?"

"Someone is following you? Please make sure no harm comes to my daughter."

"I don't plan to let anyone be harmed. The guy is more of a nuisance than anything else. But it might be wise not to lead him to your daughter's door, just in case."

"I'll see what I can do on my end. I can be persuasive when I have to be."

I wondered what Janet Maxwell meant to do. I hoped she would be discreet and not do anything that would get us all killed.

"Perhaps you should wait 'til you hear from me, Mrs. Maxwell. As soon as I know more, I'll let you know."

"Okay, but you understand my impatience. Since my husband and son died, I've had nothing to keep me going. Now I do and look forward to hearing from you."

The conversation with Janet Maxwell made me uneasy. I don't like it when clients want to participate in my investigation. I should have insisted she not interfere. Although knowing what little I did about her, I doubted she'd heed my advice. Whom would she try to persuade, and what leverage did she have?

I packed a duffel with a few gadgets of my trade and a cooler with water and ice packs. After doing an internet search for Smoulder, Pennsylvania, I decided to take Janet Maxwell's advice and watch my back. A five-hour drive from New York City, Smoulder appeared to be a one-horse town with few viable businesses and a seedy-looking hotel.

The perfect place to disappear.

CHAPTER 13

Janet Maxwell leaned against Douglas Cain's desk, looking fresh and feminine in a fitted shantung suit, the color of pink grapefruit. The intimidating stare she leveled at the lawyer as he stood at the door to his office belied her soft image.

"Janet? When did you get here?" He'd only been gone fifteen minutes.

Cain turned to glance at the area outside his office. The waiting room was empty. Past six o'clock, the two clerks who worked for him would be gone for the day. He had no late appointments. The outer glass doors were not locked until the last person left.

He entered his office and scanned the files he'd left scattered on his desk. *Shit. Does anything look out of place? How would I know?* His face tightened with anger at the thought of her rummaging through his papers.

He rounded his desk and sat back. Crossing one leg over the other, he made an attempt to appear nonchalant about Maxwell's unannounced visit.

However, the sight of her set every nerve in his body on edge.

"What are you doing here, Janet?"

"Did you think I'd just disappear, Douglas?"

His hands shook as he pushed the files into one pile. A rush of panic ran through him when he noticed one of the folders.

"Disappear?" *If only.* "Of course not, Janet." He glanced outside his office to Mrs. Grimes' empty desk. "Where is my secretary?" His sentinel was not at her post. "Perhaps you would like some coffee."

"Spare me your cordialities. Why are you having Lucas Holt followed? Was it Todd's idea?"

Cain relaxed. At least he knew why she was there.

"So, now you admit to hiring Holt. I told you to call him off. We had a deal, and it's too late for regrets about a decision you made nearly two decades ago."

"A decision would indicate choice. You gave me no choice."

Cain grimaced. "Janet, do we have to rehash all of this over and over? In the past, you were barely interested in any of the reports I gave you about your daughter. Remember, I contacted you each time. You never once called me to ask for information."

Janet moved away to face the office window. The lawyer took the opportunity to slide one of the files into his desk and lock the drawer. Maxwell spoke.

"Why should I call you when I knew we would routinely meet twice a year? Would it have done any good to ask about my child more often than that?"

"I rather think it was more a case of not wanting your husband to learn your secret. As long as you had your place in society and were taken care of, you had no use for the girl."

Janet twisted back to Cain, her arms crossed under her breasts.

"That's ridiculous, Douglas. I've always cared about my daughter."

Sensing her feigned indignation, the lawyer leaned forward, a flash of fire in his eyes.

"The only thing you care about is having some kind of hold over Todd Grayson. You've never forgiven him for choosing his family over you. Let it go, Janet. If you love your daughter, don't use her as a means for revenge against the senator. She would never forgive you if she knew the truth."

Janet Maxwell's eyes hardened. Cain noticed the white-knuckled grip on her purse and knew he'd struck a nerve. He changed tack, not wanting to push her too far. The election was around the corner, and he needed to protect Grayson from a scandal.

"Look, Janet. Tell Holt you don't need his services. The girl is still a minor. Whether you find her or not, you have no legal access to her."

"I still want to know where she is even if I can't tell her who I am."

"Please, wait a while longer. When she's eighteen, I promise I'll arrange for you two to meet."

"Really? You lying son of a bitch! You've

known where she is all along."

Cain didn't react fast enough, and when he opened his mouth to deny the accusation, Maxwell put her hand up to stop him from speaking.

"Save your lies, Douglas," she said. "Holt has far more integrity than you and will tell me what I need to know." She smiled. "There will be *no* secrets between him and me."

Cain squirmed in his chair. *She looks like the cat that ate the canary.*

Janet Maxwell continued, "He's arranged a meeting with someone in Smoulder, Pennsylvania who has information as to where she is. Soon he'll know everything, and then so will I."

"You don't need to do this. I said I would help you. What can I do, Janet?"

"Nothing. I don't want you or anyone connected with you to do anything to stop Lucas Holt from giving me what I want."

CHAPTER 14

Douglas Cain cradled a glass of Martell Cordon Bleu in his hands to warm, as he gazed at the sweeping views of Central Park.

Senator Todd Grayson entered the room carrying the aroma of a Cohiba Behike, a mix of cedar and chocolate. He held out a cigar to Cain.

"Cuba's best in my opinion, Douglas. Try one. I've already cut it."

"Then you leave me no choice." Cain took the cigar. He didn't bother to inspect it; he was sure the quality was superb. Bringing the cigar to his lips, he leaned forward to let the senator light it. Grayson held the flame steady while the lawyer puffed and rotated the tightly rolled bundle of tobacco until it glowed. Velvet smoke rose between them.

Cain looked at the tip of burning ash. "Well done, thank you."

"You're welcome. We make a good team. Isn't that right?"

"Yes, sir."

"You've   always   been   there   for   me,

Douglas…still are, I hope."

The lawyer shifted his stance. He turned back to the floor-to-ceiling windows. The russet sunset predicted a clear day ahead, if the old adage was right. But Cain sensed a storm brewing. He swirled the warm brandy and sipped it.

Grayson settled into a soft leather club chair, one of two in his study.

"My numbers are very good. I've waited a long time for this."

Cain drained his glass and crossed the room to where Grayson sat. Summoned to the senator's Central Park South apartment, just steps from the Plaza Hotel, Cain wondered what he had to say that couldn't be said in their daily phone conversation. *What pile of shit do I have to pull him out of now?*

"Is there some delicate business we need to talk about, Senator?"

"Senator? Come on, Douglas. How long have we known each other?"

"A very long time. Is something on your mind?"

Grayson rose from his chair, leaving his drink and cigar on a side table. He walked to stand in front of Cain, who, intimidated by the senator's closeness, allowed cigar ashes to fall onto the floor. He moved to clean them from the carpet but stopped when Grayson laid a heavy hand on his shoulder and squeezed.

"Leave it. We have something more important to worry about."

The pressure of Todd Grayson's grip was paralyzing. Cain could do nothing but wait for Grayson to speak again.

"Douglas…can you tell me *why* Janet Maxwell's goddamned name is on the list of donors attending my fundraiser?"

Cain thought he'd sink to the floor from the shock and weight of Grayson's arm. He was relieved when the senator removed the hold on his shoulder to take a phone call. He gave Grayson some privacy and moved to another room.

Janet Maxwell's name is on the donor list?

He couldn't believe she had donated ten thousand dollars to attend the fundraising dinner at the Plaza. As far as Cain knew, she had never been political. Her husband, yes. He was a large contributor to whichever party or politician benefited his own interests. Cain's last meeting with Janet Maxwell had caused him concern, and he knew she couldn't be trusted.

What is that sly bitch up to?

Burdened by all that was happening, Cain dragged himself back to Grayson's study. His shoulder ached and his palms were clammy. He pressed his clenched fist to his chest, which tightened with every short breath.

I feel like I'm having a heart attack.

The senator was at his desk, writing. He finished and gave Cain his attention.

"Douglas, you look like shit. Is there something more going on here?"

Cain swallowed, only able to gather a drop of saliva to moisten his throat. *God, I hate this fucking job.*

"It's Janet Maxwell. She's hired Lucas Holt to find her daughter—your daughter."

Todd Grayson sprang from his chair. "How dare you." Anger contorted his face. "How dare you mention that child to me! I don't have a daughter—I have a wife and two sons. That's my only family."

"I understand how you feel, Todd, but—"

"No! You have no idea—no idea how a rumor like that could ruin my chances for election. First the Rand bullshit and now this. I trusted you to take care of it. What the fuck happened?"

"I did what I could, and it was under control. But since Janet's husband and son died, she's felt a need to see her daughter."

"Whatever you did, Douglas, it wasn't enough." Grayson shouted, "I want this buried. Do you understand me? I don't care how you do it. I already told you I don't want to know. Just, fucking *bury it*."

Overwhelmed by Grayson's anger and the gravity of the situation, Cain only nodded and turned to leave. Before he could escape the room, Grayson leveled the final blow to Cain's tenuous position with his calm, measured command.

"Douglas, I want the issue dead."

***

"Aren't you coming to bed?" Roberta Cain asked her husband. "You've been in that chair for hours. Is there something you want to talk about?"

Douglas Cain smiled at his wife of twenty-five years. She leaned on the doorframe and folded her arms under her breasts to hold closed the thin, silky robe she wore. He knew underneath was one of the short lacy nightgowns he favored. His eyes traveled to the rise of soft flesh that peeked out when she shifted her weight off the jamb. They rested there a moment and then moved the length of her long neck to her face. Ignoring her questioning stare, he admired her hair. The beautiful auburn shade complemented her green eyes. He wanted to lose himself in them.

"Douglas?"

"No, Bobbie, it's just the usual."

"Seems more than the usual. What's that, your third drink tonight?"

Cain raised the glass and drank the last of the scotch. He shook his head and placed the empty glass on the end table. "Go back to bed, Bobbie. I'll be there soon."

"Soon it will be time to get up. Well, I need to sleep even if you don't. I have an early meeting tomorrow."

A workaholic like himself, his wife dedicated long hours to her job as a dean at Columbia University. She minored in psychology, which prompted her to question his moods. He'd been successful so far in keeping most of what was troubling about his job to himself. It was becoming harder and harder to do.

"Okay, I won't be long."

Roberta left the room, taking the sweet, musky scent of her favorite perfume with her. At first, the overpowering fragrance bothered him, but then he'd accepted it as part of her presence. Now, it was a reminder she was near. He found comfort in the strong jasmine smell. Cain listened to the fading pit-pat of his wife's slippers on the bare wood floors, replaced by lonely silence. He wished he could sleep.

Cain had to do something. Glick didn't have the capabilities to stop Holt from locating Maxwell's daughter. He'd been naïve to think the small-town police officer could handle a case as sensitive as one involving a candidate for the presidency of the United States.

The five drinks he'd had since the late dinner he and Roberta shared should have rendered him comatose, but Todd Grayson's words gripped his mind like a vise.

"...I want the issue dead."

CHAPTER 15

John Crocker, AKA Paladin, lay hunched down deep in Mexican sand with his shoulders against a palm tree.

At six foot five inches tall, it was the only way to hide his large frame. A bush hat with mosquito netting hid long black hair pulled back with a rubber band. Crocker had the rough, craggy face that appeared as if pockmarked by shrapnel. A watertight case, buried in the sand, had protected his AK-47 and Heckler & Koch sniper rifle on the swim to the beach.

He glanced up at the waxing crescent moon and clear, dark sky. *It's not ideal, but it would still be dark enough to approach the villa unseen—if I'm careful.*

Five more minutes passed, and he checked his watch for the third time. *Fifteen minutes until the changing of the guard.* The coral villa was enormous by most standards, but then the drug trade was lucrative, and Pappy could afford it.

With a little time to kill, Crocker's mind

wandered to events that brought him here. Long ago, he realized Delta Force operative skills—sniper, explosives, and communications—did not provide him job opportunities.

He had been honest with himself; Crocker admitted he missed "the life." His heart wasn't into being head of security, sitting behind a desk from nine to five.

A fellow ex-member of Delta Force had recruited him to become a mercenary. He didn't need much convincing; the money was excellent, the assignments short, and he could reject any job that didn't suit him. Perhaps best of all, someone he never met screened clients, and he would receive assignments via a drop. Plausible deniability up and down. Crocker thought of himself as a small business owner who didn't pay taxes.

The drop he received a day ago provided details on Crocker's current target: a photo of Pappy Maldonado, some data on his drug operation, his location, and a complete description of the villa and guards. No time for assignment completion specified. No expectations as to results meant to eliminate the threat.

The file detailed exact guard movements; two guards in the front and two in the back rotated position every two hours. One pair would not communicate with the other unless there was a problem. As agreed, he destroyed the file after memorizing it.

With three minutes remaining, Crocker opened the case and removed the H&K sniper rifle. He had pre-adjusted the stock length and the cheek piece vertically. He attached the Brugger and Thomet silencer and the lighter five-round magazine. Crocker only needed two shots. The H&K kicked the cartridge case ten meters. If you worried about giving away your position to return fire, you chose a different weapon.

He rolled over and focused through his scope at the two guards on the second floor. The one to Crocker's right entered the house.

Fuck. Why didn't the other one leave too? At that moment, the guard flicked away his cigarette and followed his *compadre*. In three minutes, the replacements would arrive.

Crocker set down the H&K and removed his AK-47 from its case. Operating in sandy, windy weather, he preferred his Kalash, for its ability to withstand large amounts of foreign matter and not failing to recycle. It was a reliable weapon and he accepted some loss of accuracy. He inserted a loaded magazine, pulled back, and released the charging handle. He carried several thirty-round magazines providing him more than enough ammunition for automatic fire. He set it down on the case and returned to the H&K.

Two new guards strolled out and lit cigarettes. They fell into a pattern of pacing back and forth on the terrace. Crocker waited until they met in the middle and turned. He made a minor adjustment to the Hensoldt scope, aimed and fired. *Pfffft.* The head of the guard to Crocker's right exploded, spraying the walls with blood, bone, and brain matter. The cigarette fell from the mouth of the second guard as he spun around and lurched back.

Crocker panned his movement and when the guard froze, he fired again. The headless body slammed against the wall and toppled forward.

After Crocker placed the sniper rifle back in the case and buried it in the sand, he grabbed the AK-47. He paused to be sure no one responded to the shooting. The only thing he heard were ocean waves lapping the shore.

The remote location ensured no one would see him scuttle toward the villa in the dark. He rose, brought the AK-47 to his chin, and crab-walked from one palm tree to the next, reaching a patio door.

Crocker opened a case attached to his khaki web belt and took out a roll of tape and a glasscutter attached to a string. Holding the string to the edge of the door, he scribed a semi-circle in the glass adjacent to the lock. Placing tape over the semi-circle, he gently tapped the glass until it came loose and removed it. He bent over at the hole and listened for a moment; it was as quiet as a tomb. Crocker wiped away beads of sweat from his forehead, reached in, and unlocked the door. He pulled a small can of WD-40 from his web belt and sprayed around the edges. It opened quietly.

A cool blast of air conditioning made Crocker grin. Taking out a flashlight, he entered a large dark room. Most of the space was set up as a den with a television, sectional sofa, and a pool table. A small area displayed framed news articles about Pappy Maldonado, describing him as "Mr. Untouchable," "Mexico's Cruelest Man," and "The Power behind the Cartel." Crocker advanced to an open door. He jutted his head out, looked both ways, and found the stairs up, to his right.

The intelligence he received indicated Pappy rarely traveled and ran his business through couriers from home. The villa had been watched from a fishing boat for a week. There was only one roaming guard when Pappy wasn't home.

Crocker crouched, testing each step as he climbed to the main part of the villa. He inched his head above the top step. He saw a luxurious living room straight ahead with fine artwork and a hallway to other rooms. Another step up, he turned his head to the left, spotting the leg of a dead guard through the patio door. Looking to the right, he saw the kitchen entrance.

Still dead quiet throughout.

Entering the living room, Crocker took two steps toward the hallway when a scream startled him. *Shit.*

A tall, shapely girl in a black teddy shot back to the kitchen, forcing Crocker to follow. He stuck his head in and pulled it out as a butcher's knife swooped down. *It didn't take long for her to grow some balls.* Crocker lunged past her into the kitchen, turned, and shot her, center mass. Her stunned expression relaxed in death as her body slid to the floor.

I'm not taking prisoners—not even pretty young girls.

Crocker heard yelling in Spanish between three people. Pappy and the other two guards were down the hallway. They called, "Pablo! Juan!"

Their shouts told Crocker they were approaching

the living room. It would only take a moment for them to find him alone in the kitchen. *Okay. Now, they know it's just the three of them. One small advantage I have is they don't know I'm the only hostile they face.*

"Delta One, this is Delta Four!" Crocker yelled. "Now! Now! NOW!"

Alarmed, the guards swiveled their semi-automatic rifles left and right to see from which direction the attack was coming. Crocker set the fire selector switch on the AK-47 to automatic and stepped from the kitchen to confront the two guards. He fired two short bursts before they could get off a shot.

Once again, the house was silent.

Crocker loaded a fresh clip into his weapon. *Pappy's smart. He didn't leave with the guards. He knew the hammer would fall on them, and he'd learn more about the threat.* Crocker was losing time. A walker or drive-by may have heard the shots.

Hurrying to the edge of the hallway, he stepped over the dead guards. He took a moment to listen and ran to the first door to find an empty bathroom. He hurried to the second and third doors and found empty bedrooms. One room left—the master bedroom.

He kicked open the door and stepped out of the way, expecting gunfire, but was greeted with more silence. He entered, pointed his AK-47, and fired into the closed closet and the bathroom. No Pappy. *Where is this fucker?*

A deep rumbling sound drew his attention and

the pieces fell into place.

The garage door is opening.

Pappy had slipped out the window, leaped to the patio, ran around front, and entered the garage. As Crocker ran downstairs and out the front door, he heard the roar of a large SUV. A black Escalade exploded from the garage. Crocker, facing the left side of the garage, knew Pappy would be unable to shoot at him from the driver's side, while he could fire into the front windshield and side window.

Crocker aimed.

Pappy turned the heavy SUV toward Crocker and accelerated.

He could see the gray shadow of Pappy's head. He stood his ground and emptied the clip.

The Cadillac missed Crocker by scant inches when he dove out of the way.

The out-of-control vehicle veered off the driveway and slammed into a stone retaining wall. Crocker jumped up, ignoring a bruised shoulder and a gash in his leg.

He threw the AK-47 over his good shoulder, drew his Glock, and hobbled to the driver's side. Pappy's face looked like hamburger. His V-neck T-shirt was bright red.

Congratulations, Pappy, you're my thirtieth.

Crocker's phone vibrated in his pocket. He stared at the number, a number he had not seen in years and answered. "What?"

"Paladin. It's Cain."

CHAPTER 16

"Cain, call this number again in forty-five."

Talk about bad timing.

Crocker ran to the beach, retrieved his case containing the H&K sniper rifle, and returned to the villa. His original plan was to drive off in the beautiful Escalade but that idea was shot to hell with Pappy.

In the living room, he searched two of the guards and found car keys for a Chevrolet Impala. It took him less than five minutes to be on the road, passing *la policia* racing in the opposite direction with sirens blaring and red and blue roof lights piercing the night.

***

Back in his hotel room, Crocker toweled off, picked out a pair of tan slacks and a tropical silk shirt. He finished dressing when his phone rang.

"Yeah."

"Paladin, thank God."

"For what? You must be in some deep shit if you're calling me after all these years. I thought the statute of limitations ran out on that little favor I owed you."

"Little? You ungrateful bastard, I—"

Crocker heard the slur in Cain's speech.

"Relax, counselor. You sound shit-faced. Maybe you should call me back once you've dried out. By the way, I don't use that name anymore—too many bad memories. I'm Crocker now."

"I'm f…fine, and I don't give a fuck what you call yourself." Cain's harsh whisper came through the phone. "I have a job for you."

"You mean you want me to return the favor."

"Never mind the favor—I can pay."

"Now I know you're drunk."

"Pal—Crocker, you're pissing me off."

"Whoa, don't want to do that," Crocker quipped. "This must be big. Anything to do with Mr. High and Mighty?"

"This is no joke…no fucking joke. Do you…understand?"

"Yeah, okay, tell me what you need."

"I have two problems that require your special attention," Cain said. "I want you in Broome, Pennsylvania ASAP."

"How much attention? I don't usually ask for too many details, but since you have friends in high places, I have to know what I'm getting myself into."

"I'll leave the details to your discretion. The first problem is a young woman. Her name is Karen Martin." Cain paused and Crocker could hear what sounded like the lawyer swallowing a drink. "She lives in Broome with her adoptive parents. Someone is looking for her, and I don't want her found."

"Are you asking me to do what I think you are?"

"No. I need you to isolate her until my second problem is resolved."

"Which is?"

"The person hired to search for the girl is a New York City PI."

Crocker planned to check out the hotel bar for some companionship. He moved to a mirrored chest and grabbed a comb, sliding it through his damp hair. "C'mon, I haven't got all night. Who's the PI?"

"Lucas Holt."

Crocker raised his head to the mirror and stared at his reflection. His jaw clenched at the memory associated with that name. His disfigured face flushed with anger. Lost in the past, he flinched when Cain shouted into the phone.

"Are you there, Crocker?"

"Yeah."

"Is this a problem for you?"

"Of course not."

***

After a bout of rough and satisfying sex with the first hooker he could engage, Crocker packed up and drove his rented car to Cancun International Airport. He boarded the private jet Cain had arranged for him and within seven hours, using GPS, Crocker drove into Broome, Pennsylvania.

CHAPTER 17

Crocker moved through the pines and ash, stopping at the edge of the woods. He stared at the decaying red barn topped by a Witch's Hat cupola. The roof remained intact, except for patches of worn shingles, exposing the cedar underneath. Much of the paint had weathered and chipped away.

At one time, someone cared enough to put a copper rooster weather vane on the gambrel roof, the detail of its form obscured by a bright green patina. Dutch doors hung with loosened hinges on both sides of the barn. Huge sliding panels dominated the front. The doors in the hayloft, like all the others, were nailed shut.

Using a wonder bar he had in his truck, he pried loose the nails on one of the Dutch doors and entered. Crocker scanned the spacious interior. Protected from the elements, the inside had survived years of neglect. Five horse stalls and a tack room lined a long wall. Crocker ascended the ship's ladder at the center of the barn to the loft. The rusted pulleys used to lift bales of hay were still at the loft door, but broken. Five trap doors in the floor allowed hay to drop to each stall below.

What was important to Crocker was the beam. He walked a few feet along the solid piece of timber and determined it would hold the weight he had in mind. He climbed down and exited the barn.

Hidden by the heavy thicket of trees that edged Farm Road sat a ranch house. Crocker guessed it had been built in the 1940s, and by the amount of damage and neglect, was unoccupied for at least twenty years. Although among the first places searched when looking for a missing person, he liked abandoned properties. There, he could move about freely preparing for his mission. He especially liked *old* abandoned properties. They almost always yielded surprises. Crocker soon discovered this one was no exception.

The inside of the house was much the same as the outside, crumbling, and a haven for feral animals when winter came. He exited through the kitchen door, which hung by one hinge, and scanned the backyard beyond a clump of oaks. An overgrowth of tall grasses and weeds hid any evidence of a garden or lawn.

Someone had called this place home. A fleeting memory of his youth and an unfamiliar stab of pain surged through the professional killer. His body tensed, and he pushed the thought aside. Anger and coldness had long ago replaced pain.

Crocker didn't have a real home—he didn't need or want one. He was a loner and an assassin whose work kept him on the move. If he had a prolonged period of down time or needed to flee, he had a place in Morocco where he could go.

He walked the back of the property, canvassing the ground as he moved. Crocker grinned when he came upon a four-foot square area of matted leaves and dirt, covered with large twigs and branches. It appeared something kept the grasses and weeds from growing. He kicked away the wood pieces and brushed the leaves and dirt to the side. Crocker stomped his boot on what lay underneath and heard a hollow sound.

Removing more debris, he exposed the perimeter of a trap door. Its rusty hinges creaked as he pulled on a handle, revealing a darkened space.

He shone a light inside. A half dozen crudely built steps led to an underground storage area. He descended the steps. The room was no more than six feet deep and the size of a large closet. The few shelves against the wall were empty but for one sealed glass jar that contained something unrecognizable.

A root cellar.

Another unpleasant memory flashed through Crocker's mind. He climbed the steps and slammed the door shut.

***

Crocker hiked for an hour, looking for evidence of trails made by campers or signs someone had passed through. There were no boot prints or litter anywhere.

This place is pristine.

The area, with its many tall trees, rocky hills, and

valleys, had the feeling of being untouched by anyone in years. Sharp blades of sunlight stabbed through the high canopy of leaves and landed on dead pine needles as far as the eye could see.

Between a row of evergreen shrubs and a steep incline at the base of the mountain lay a secluded area that suited his purpose.

No one would pass this way.

Crocker dropped his backpack, pulled a compact military shovel from its web loop, and began digging the first of two graves.

CHAPTER 18

Karen Martin was glad her parents had decided to go to Virginia to visit Uncle Joe and give her some space.

Her mother's brother was an odd sort who was divorced and worked at a tobacco company. Karen thought the only reason her mother visited Joe was to make sure he didn't run the house Sarah and Joe inherited into ruins. At least moving to Pennsylvania made for an easier drive.

She knew it was hard for them to leave her alone.

Sarah Martin, slim, fair-haired, and dressed for summer in white shorts and a pink tee, wrung her hands as she spoke.

"Honey, are you sure you're gonna be okay here by yourself?"

Karen smiled at the woman who, as far as she knew, had given birth to her seventeen and a half years before. The family had always been inseparable. Now, Sarah and Daniel were leaving her alone for the first time.

"C'mon, Mom, of course I am. I have to get used

to doing things on my own. I'll be going to college in a few weeks."

Karen attributed Sarah's recent weepiness to Karen's acceptance into Temple, where she would attend in the fall. At the mention of college, Sarah's eyes became watery. Karen pushed aside her own anxiety about leaving home. She knew they would all adjust. They had been too dependent on each other. When Karen was young, she loved the constant attention from her parents. Except for school, she was rarely without them. But as she grew older, their devotion began to suffocate her. Karen never had the heart to tell them. She loved them dearly and thought all parents were the same.

"Mary's coming to visit, remember? Technically, I won't be alone. I'm so excited to see her."

Wiping a stray tear, Sarah nodded. "I know, sweetheart. You're all grown up now. I can't believe how fast the time has gone by."

Karen stood six inches over her mother and was nearly as tall as her father, who was average height at five foot ten. Both Sarah and Daniel had brown eyes and as Karen grew older, she had wondered aloud how she could be as tall as her mother at only twelve. How odd to be the only one in the family with blue eyes. Not serious, she would sometimes tease her parents that they must have found her on their doorstep like a certain fictional wizard. They would laugh and hug her and tell her how silly she was. She never caught the guilty glance that passed between Sarah and Daniel when she'd turned away.

Growing up in Vermont, Karen loved its mountain vistas, rolling hills and the farms along

Lake Champlain. Daniel, trim and athletic had taught her to ski. They kayaked on the lake, biked along trails, and camped in the woods. When she was thirteen, she and her parents moved from Shelburne to Stowe.

Entering high school, Karen found it difficult to make new friends. Even though most students had already formed cliques, Barbara Hansen and Mary Wells hadn't belonged to any group, and the three became fast friends. Since moving to Broome, Karen had only kept in touch with Mary and Jason, her ex-boyfriend.

Once they moved to Broome, Daniel and Sarah Martin spent more time with each other and less time with their daughter. Karen supposed it was their way of cutting the cord.

She had started to date a boy recently—one of a group who liked to camp off Moose Horn Trail. Karen hadn't told her parents yet. *One drama at a time.*

Daniel and Sarah had packed the car early that morning and woke Karen to see them off. She hugged and kissed her parents. "Have a great time. Tell Uncle Joe I said hello." She noticed her mother's trembling lips, looked at her father, and frowned. Daniel Martin put an arm around his wife, coaxing her into the car.

"Let's go, Sarah, it's only for a few days. It's not like we'll never see her again."

Karen smiled as her father pulled her into a tight hug and then slipped into the driver's seat and drove away.

***

Enjoying some alone time, Karen stood on the back porch, holding her orange cat. Oliver purred and Karen sighed at the cloudless sky. *It's a great day to be outdoors.*

Oliver must have sensed Mary's arrival before the bell rang. He jumped out of Karen's arms, taking off toward the steep hill at the back of the house. Karen ran inside through the kitchen and living room and yanked open the front door.

So much alike physically, she and Mary Wells could have been sisters. It may have been what drew them together, that and the fact that neither had siblings. Karen was amused that she resembled Mary's parents, who were tall with light hair and eyes, more than she did her own.

Mary greeted Karen with a squeal and a crushing hug. Mr. and Mrs. Wells sat in their car and waved to Karen. She jogged down the walk to see them.

"You girls have fun," Mrs. Wells said. "Karen, tell your parents we said hi. We'll be back this way probably the middle of next week."

Mary Wells threw her parents a kiss and waved goodbye. When they drove away, she wrapped Karen in another crushing hug.

"C'mon," Karen said. "Let's go inside. I'll tell you all about the fantastic stuff I've got planned."

"No, tell me about your boyfriend."

Karen rolled her eyes. "Sam's not exactly a boyfriend. He's one of the guys we camp with. We hooked up a few times."

"Sounds like a boyfriend to me. Are we going camping?"

Karen nodded. "Camping is so cool here. All the

kids our age are into it. The campsites are great, and as you get up into the mountains, the views are to *die* for."

CHAPTER 19

After an hour of driving in the hills of Broome, Pennsylvania, Crocker found a dirt road partially concealed by weeds and climbing vines. He parked between two pine trees, keeping the blazing hot sun from heating up the rented black Ford pickup.

Opening the fiberglass camper shell, he found his backpack and removed a pair of high-powered binoculars, a tripod, and two energy bars. Leaving the pickup, he walked thirty feet to the edge of the hill, sat and looked down at the back of 26 Adams Street. He planned to spend the afternoon and evening watching the Martin home.

Crocker's cell phone emitted a soft tone. *What could he want now?* "Cain, you can't ring me up anytime you want when I'm on an assignment. Your timing usually sucks."

There was a long pause, and then Cain responded, "Did you locate her? Have you got a plan?"

Crocker let out an impatient breath. "Yeah. I have surveillance set up now. I found an abandoned farm that will be perfect for what I have in mind."

"Holt's on his way to Pennsylvania."

Crocker smiled. "Good."

"Don't underestimate him."

"Don't underestimate me. Wouldn't it have been easier to take care of him in New York?"

"No. I don't want you anywhere near here. I don't know what you're going to do, but make sure it doesn't find its way back to me. When do you think you'll be done?"

"Shit, Cain, I don't know. This process is fluid. I make my decisions when it makes the most sense. You sent me here with little information. I have to gather my own intel and be ready to move on a moment's notice."

"Okay, fine. Call me as soon it's finished."

"You'll know when it's finished."

"Crocker, remember your priorities. You need to keep the girl and her family away from Holt. I don't care how you deal with him."

"Don't tell me how to do my job, Cain. And my priority is to accomplish the goal with no personal casualty. I'll do whatever is necessary."

"What does that mean? Don't harm the girl, Crocker."

Ignoring Cain, he attached the binoculars to the tripod and pointed it at the white saltbox.

"Crocker, are you listening to me?"

"I'm done talking to you. Don't call me again," Crocker said and shut off the phone.

***

He saw one car in the driveway at the side of the house and lights on inside. Crocker sat back, took a bite of an energy bar, and let his mind wander.

John Crocker had been a Green Beret for four years when he joined Delta Force. It was the proudest day of his life. There were twelve hundred members in the invitation-only, elite organization.

After completing training, his team was chosen to participate in a weekend exercise. The goal was simple: capture the flag of the opposing team. The rules and the playing field were not simple. The game was conducted at night on a five-mile grid of hills and valleys. Each team knew the starting position of the opponent and the location of the flag, but the flag could be moved once within a half mile of the starting position.

All combatants were fitted with MILES— Multiple Integrated Laser Engagement Systems. A laser transmitter fitted to each rifle mimicked the range of the weapon when fired. Each soldier wore minute receivers on different parts of the body. When a player was "killed," the receiving device emitted a loud tone that turned off by using a special key in the soldier's possession. At that time, he removed himself from the game. There were referees at several points monitoring the competition. The teams did not physically engage each other; they used stealth.

Crocker's DF1 team was comprised of Green Berets invited to join Delta Force. The team studied terrain maps and strategized the entire week. As squad leader, Crocker had decided to employ a routine of marching twenty feet apart and maintaining radio silence. He moved the red flag from their base camp to the half-mile perimeter and placed it high in a tree. While the terrain maps were helpful, he preferred to walk the field one night before the exercise to choose the best route. These strategies weren't against the rules, but it defied the spirit of the game.

At first, the war game proceeded as expected; both teams advanced without a hitch. Crocker led the DF1 team two and a half miles to the halfway marker. Entering an area of dense trees and brush, he halted and stretched both arms out telling his team to kneel.

Crocker heard a disturbing whirring that wasn't there the night before. Making eye contact with team members on either side of him, he signed, "Cover me." He watched as the sign was repeated down the line and then moved forward, slow and silent.

If team DF6 is ahead, they aren't drawing a breath.

Crocker took two paces forward. The low drone escalated to a loud hum. He brushed against a shrub, provoking an angry horde of hornets to fill the air and attack every inch of his exposed skin. His arms spazzed as he tried to wave off the frenzied insects and pull mosquito netting from his bush hat over his face. Crocker struggled not to make a sound. All his team could do was watch in horror as their leader's face began to swell.

Moments later, his pain and humiliation deepened when Crocker's MILES alarm shrieked as a Delta Force 6 operative tagged him. He staggered off the field of engagement, swearing under his breath.

A DF6 member snickered in the brush, giving away his location. Three of Crocker's DF1 teammates converged on him. At that moment, the rest of DF6 silently circled them and, after combat crawling a safe distance, broke into a run to the DF1 base.

The DF6 snickering decoy was tagged. Thinking there were more DF6 soldiers ahead, Crocker's team maintained cover and advanced. Thirty minutes had passed by the time they reached their opponent's base camp. Three DF1 team members were instructed to break cover and pursue someone running in the opposite direction, carrying a blue flag. They lost their prey twice before picking him up again. Team DF1 surrounded and trapped him at the perimeter of the DF6 base camp.

Lucas Holt, Army Ranger, now Delta Force 6 squad leader waved a fake flag that read, **'Green Berets are a bunch of Wussies.'**

Delta Force 6, alone at the opposition's base, used flashlights and found the flag in the tree.

Crocker had walked the route the night before. There was no hornet nest. He still scratched the facial scars, still knew the anguish and embarrassment of leaving his squad on the field, and always suspected Lucas Holt had placed the hornets' nest in their path.

Holt's gonna pay.

CHAPTER 20

By noon I headed out of the city, west through New Jersey on I-78, and within an hour and a half passed over the Delaware River into Pennsylvania. Unlike the winding northern route through the Pocono Mountains, moderate hills flanked the relatively mundane interstate highway. Once past Harrisburg, I picked up the turnpike, traveling through small to medium-sized towns, state forests, parks, and game lands.

Although my ultimate destination was Smoulder, I exited the turnpike at Somerset, twenty minutes away. I checked into one of the local hotel chains and inquired about renting a vehicle. Speedy Car & Truck Rental was a fifteen-minute walk from the hotel. I called ahead to see if they had what I wanted, which they did, and grabbed a Starbucks on the way there. Forty-five *slow* minutes later, I pulled a nondescript gray truck with local plates next to my Rover and transferred a few items to the rental. I brought the rest, my suitcase, duffel, and laptop to the room.

By the time I'd eaten, showered, and dressed, I had little more than an hour before meeting Daniel Martin. The weather channel forecasted clear skies and an evening temperature of fifty-seven degrees. I wore boot-cut jeans, a black golf shirt and sports jacket, and leather desert boots.

As I locked my laptop and personal effects in the room safe, my cell rang. The number was vaguely familiar.

"Hello?"

"Mr. Holt, this is Kathryn Sullivan. You left a message on my answering machine."

"Yes, thank you for returning my call."

"I have to say your note and message were a bit unsettling. I've never spoken to a private investigator before. You want to know about the Martins. Has something happened?"

"As far as I know the Martins are fine. I just need to locate them regarding a business matter. I was told they moved to Pennsylvania. Do you happen to know specifically where?"

"No, we didn't have any personal conversations with them. We only talked about the house. I know the daughter was planning to go to school in Pennsylvania."

"Yes, I know. Is there anything else you can remember? Sometimes idle chitchat yields information. It could be something you overheard them saying among themselves."

She was silent for a few seconds.

"No, nothing I can recall."

"What about their mail? I imagine they arranged for the post office to forward their mail. Any conversations about that with the mailman?"

"No, we hardly ever see him. We're usually working."

I could hear her sigh.

"Sorry I can't be more help."

I was disappointed the call was a dead end and didn't want to waste any more time. I had an appointment to keep.

"Thank you again, Mrs. Sullivan, for taking the time to call me. Of course, if you think of—"

"Oh wait, I just remembered. We received a package shortly after we moved in. I had to take it to the post office so they could forward it."

I didn't see the significance of what she was telling me. If delivered to her home, then the address on the package would be the Martins' former one. I checked the time. It was after seven.

"Was there something about the package you think would be helpful to me? Do you remember who sent it? Was it from an individual or a business?"

I thought I might trace their new address through another person or business.

"No, I don't remember who sent the package. But there was definitely something about it that sticks in my mind."

"Okay, I have to go, but if you think of anything else, please let me know. Anything at all. A place or a name."

"That's it!" Kathryn Sullivan shouted into the phone.

"What?"

"The name of the town on the package. The

number of the house and street were correct as well as the state and zip code. I guess that's why it was delivered. I remember our regular mailman was on vacation. We were getting a lot of the Martins' mail. But the name of the town was crossed out. It wasn't Stowe. It was Broome."

***

A quick internet search verified there was indeed a Broome, Pennsylvania. Still intent on keeping my date with Daniel Martin, I slipped a burner phone and a wallet with some cash and an expired driver's license into my jacket pocket. I like to have ID on me, but not knowing what situation I was walking into, I'd rather not chance losing anything too valuable. Setting my personal phone to silent, I strapped it on my left leg at the knee. My .38 special rested snugly in a holster at my right ankle.

At 7:25 p.m. I drove the rented truck southwest to Smoulder.

A faded sign, swinging on one rusty chain and boasting an establishment date of 1870, stood at the town limits. I should have suggested Mr. Martin and I meet at high noon. To describe Smoulder as rundown would be an understatement. Two deserted gas stations, one on each corner, marked the entrance to Park Street. Dusty, littered sidewalks with chipped curbs and weeds sprouting through cracks presented a poor first impression and didn't live up to its name.

The two-lane main drag ran straight-as-an-arrow, seven blocks end to end. One-story commercial buildings on both sides of the first two streets housed a hardware store, a small grocery convenience store, an insurance agency, and a cigar shop. Early twentieth-century row houses, some with abandoned first-floor shops, faced each other across Park Street for another two blocks. I could see to the cross street at the end, which was backed by wooded hills.

Gunslinger's Saloon occupied the first floor of a fire-singed brick building. Plywood boards covered the second and third story windows of the corner row house. Cars and pickups filled half the lot on the side of the building.

No one entered or exited as I passed by and took the second left down Clover Lane. The streets off Park, named for foliage, constituted the residential area of Smoulder, a scattering of two-story frame houses and empty lots. I didn't see a municipal building, police or fire station, or a school. In fact, I didn't see a soul as I drove up and down the side streets.

Back on Park, I cruised to the end of town. A bank wedged between two old houses was the only place of activity. Patrons, mostly men in tattered jeans, graphic tees, and work boots, streamed in and out. I couldn't help thinking it was payday and I'd see most of them down at the saloon. I wanted to leave the truck in a public place and found the best I could do was the bank.

Parking near the only light in the lot, I left the key fob in the truck, locked it with a spare key, and dropped it in a nearby planter. If someone planned an ambush, without a key fob on my person, he wouldn't find my truck. At ten to eight, I made my way to the Gunslinger's Saloon. The streetlights that lined the main street gave off a dull glow. Smoulder was a town that could only improve with darkness. I thought it was too bad I'd be there to see it.

I could hear Johnny Cash singing "Ring of Fire" before pulling open the dark glass door. The inside was what you would expect from the outside: long and narrow, run down, mismatched tables and chairs, and a bar that looked homemade. There were country album covers on the wall. Despite the gruff decor, Gunslinger's Saloon attracted both sexes. I grabbed the lone open stool at the corner of the bar and ordered a beer. I was wary about meeting a stranger in a seedy bar, at night, in a neighborhood that had seen much better days.

Glancing around, everyone was paired with dates or spouses except two men standing at the opposite end of the bar. One bearded and one bald. I could only observe them from the chest up. Beard was thin and had a scruffy goatee. His frayed farmer's shirt was missing a breast pocket. Beady eyes darted in my direction and back to his beer.

If I had to bet on which one was the alpha male, it would be Bald. His round face was clean-shaven and his lips were set in a permanent frown. He wore a clean, pressed, western-style shirt, which clung to his barrel chest. Bald divided his attention between a scantily clad woman with thin, bleached hair and me. I made a mental note to see if they became too interested in what I did.

Johnny Cash gave way to Lee Greenwood

singing "God Bless the USA." The crowd began rocking and singing when a new customer walked in. He scanned the bar and picked me out, approaching with a grin on his ruddy face and his hand out.

"Are you Holt?"

A worn, plaid short-sleeve shirt covered his husky frame. His shoes looked to be steel-tipped construction boots that were new ten years ago. If this was Daniel Martin, ski instructor, then I was Patsy Cline.

I needed to play along and learn what I could. I stood and shook his hand. "I'm Lucas Holt. Thanks for taking time to talk, Mr. Martin."

"Oh, sure, glad to. Call me Danny." He winced when a group seated at a table having their own private party began to hoot and howl with laughter. "Maybe we should talk outside where we can hear each other better."

If we sat in a booth, and Beard and Bald came over, I'd be trapped and unable to defend myself. Worse, if a fight ensued, the bar manager could involve the police and I'd be spending the night trying to talk myself out of jail. Outside, I knew I could eliminate them one at a time.

"Sounds good, Danny," I said. He had the wide grin of a lottery winner frozen on his face.

I twisted to leave a tip for the bartender, which allowed me to glimpse the end of the bar. Bald had lost his lustful interest in the stringy-haired blonde. Beard appeared not to notice he held an empty beer glass. This smelled like one of Glick's tricks.

I glanced back at "Danny" Martin, returning his

grin with one of my own. He walked toward the front door and I followed.

Outside, Martin turned to face me, which kept my back to the exit.

"Mr. Holt. If it's okay, you know, just to ease my mind, let's exchange some ID." Martin had his ready and extended his hand to keep me facing him. I shifted my body so I could view the exit and reached for my back pocket. A few things happened simultaneously.

The Gunslinger's Saloon door opened and Beard and Bald came through grinning as if it was their birthday. They stared at me with surprised expressions. Daniel pulled back his driver's license and attempted to put it into a slot in his wallet. With both hands occupied, for a moment in time he was helpless. I spun and kicked his right kneecap. He sucked in a quick breath as his eyes bulged. Letting out a tortured scream, he fell to the concrete. One down, two to go. I thought if I took out another, the third would quit or run.

Beard paused. He glanced in every direction before he moved again. Bald kept his confident grin and composure. Before his muscular build had turned to flab, he was probably used to getting his way. He came straight at me with a right and the intent of a knockout. He was a brawler, not a boxer. Sidestepping his tattooed arm, his punch sailed by my right shoulder. I stepped forward and stiff-arm punched his right kidney. Doubled over, he dropped to his knees, gasping in pain.

I glared at Beard.

"Uh...wait, man, I was just along for a beer," he

said, then lunged at me.

Out of the corner of my eye, I caught the rush of a dark figure before everything went black.

CHAPTER 21

Crocker stared at the black sky.

He wasn't sure of his plan. Houses were far apart, but climbing down the hill exposed him to anyone up and out past midnight. He didn't know how many people were in the house. If he entered the house, he had no idea if the floors or stairs creaked, if a pet would announce his arrival or if the girls were awake. He hated the lack of information usually provided him and his target's arbitrary movements. He liked the certainty of a routine. These girls didn't have one.

Perhaps he was being overly cautious. The barn was ready and the graves dug. Still, he hesitated.

Fuck it. No guts, no glory.

Crocker trekked down the hill, avoiding stones and holes dug by animals. He glanced up and swore. A light, which was off, was now on.

When he reached the base of the hill, he sat and surveyed the back of the house. He used his camo hat to wipe sweat from his forehead. The woods were quiet except for the occasional rustling of dead leaves and the distant hoot of an owl. Like other predators, night became his milieu, isolation and darkness his element. He sat in a semi-meditative state, feeling no emotion or empathy for the girls and what he was about to do. Crocker rose and inched toward the garage.

***

Karen Martin padded down the stairs trying not to wake Mary. Her head pounded like a sledgehammer on stone and she needed her migraine medication. She thought it would be in the usual place in the kitchen. It wasn't. Nor was it in the bathroom medicine cabinet. Catching her reflection in the mirror, she cringed at the person looking back at her with bloodshot eyes and puffy lids. *The car. I took it when we went food shopping.*

She opened the front door and stepped out. As she crossed the driveway to the car, Karen breathed in the scent of pine and listened to the night sounds. She panicked when she heard the ground crunch nearby and then remembered a pesky raccoon came nightly to scavenge through their trash. Karen retrieved her pills and returned to the kitchen, holding one hand to her forehead. She opened the refrigerator for a cold bottle of water and groaned, realizing they forgot to restock. *Why is this happening? I hope there's more in the garage.*

***

Crocker peered through layers of dust and grime on the window at the side of the attached garage. Inside were stacks of boxes, tools, two bicycles, and a door leading into the house. He tugged on the lower half of the double hung window. It didn't budge. Even if he took the time to cut the glass, unlock the window, and awkwardly climb through, there was no guarantee the door inside was unlocked. The low shrubs at the property line didn't offer enough cover. Someone might see him from the street. *Let's call this "plan B."*

***

She heard a noise. Karen paused before entering the darkened garage. After a few moments of silence, she eased open the door. Her eyes widened at seeing a shadow pass the dirty window. She relaxed, realizing it was the shrubs outside that swayed with the evening breeze. Karen turned on the light and moved to the water stacked under the windowsill. She took an armful of bottles and headed back inside.

***

Crocker stood at the back of the house and smiled at his good fortune as he raised the unlocked window and listened. It was as quiet as an old widow's home after the funeral. He opened it wider to accommodate his frame and pulled the top half of his body into a ground floor storage room. He shimmied in the rest of the way and rolled on the floor. *Good, the door's closed.* He rose from a worn rug and leaned against a cardboard box. Drawing his pistol, he attached a silencer. Crocker crept across the room. He reached for the doorknob then recoiled when something thudded against the door.

***

What was that?

Karen sat on the sofa turning the pages of a magazine. She put it aside.

I can't read or relax with this throbbing headache. Is Mary up?

She walked to the bottom of the stairs and listened, expecting her friend to come out of the bedroom. Karen waited, but the house fell quiet again. *I'm going back to bed.* She started to climb the stairs.

There it is again! A faint, soft movement came from somewhere in the house. Then stopped. She stepped down and returned to the hall. The silence of the cold house surrounded her and the isolation of the dark, narrow hallway made her shudder. She wasn't sure she wanted to investigate or race back to her room. Karen heard a soft scratching and summoning her courage, inched toward the sound. She turned the corner.

Relief washed over her when she spotted the tabby in the hallway, pawing at a closed door. "Oliver, it's you." Karen picked up the cat. "What's got you so curious?" She eased open the door. Flipping on the light, she peeked into the unused room. Odd pieces of furniture, boxes of books, and pieces of luggage stood against all the walls.

She entered and twisted slowly to scan around her. *Everything looks the same. But then I haven't been in here lately.* She let the cat out of her arms. He skulked to the window and jumped up to the sill, concealing the two-inch opening.

"Don't get comfortable, Oliver," she said. The cat ignored her and settled in. "Okay, suit yourself. I'm going to bed."

As she turned to leave, she thought she saw a movement out of the corner of her eye. The closet door was ajar. She had to check inside. She would never be able to go back upstairs otherwise. With her heart thumping in her chest, she yanked open the door and let out a sharp, stilted scream as a box fell on her. She stumbled backwards, down onto the carpet. Karen stilled and waited for someone or something to emerge. After a few agonizing, silent seconds, she rose from the floor.

And froze, feeling something brush up against her back.

The cat meowed and slunk to the closet, his tail swinging back and forth in a hunting motion. He sniffed and scratched at the stacked boxes and lifted his tail forming a question mark. Karen knew it meant the cat did not sense any danger. Seeing and hearing nothing, Karen shook off her anxiety. She scooped up the cat into her arms.

"Silly cat, there's no one there," Karen said, more to herself than to Oliver. "I'm too worked up to go back to sleep. Let's give Sam a call," she said as she settled into a chair.

***

Sonofabitch. Crocker lay on the ground, back pressed against the house. Since one of the girls was awake, he had to reconsider his strategy. He listened through the window he'd left slightly open.

***

"Yes, Sam, everything is fine. I woke up with a migraine and took my medication. I began to hear noises and couldn't go back to sleep, so I thought I'd wake you," she said with a smile.

"I was thinking...maybe, you'd like to come over." She stood up, dropping Oliver to the floor. "Mary is still asleep. No, you'll sleep on the couch." She really liked Sam, but *it* was not going to happen...yet. "Tomorrow? Mary and I are going camping. I'll take her to our usual place off Moose Horn Trail." Sam had found a secluded campsite off the beaten path, away from the main sites. "Okay. Five minutes. I'll be waiting." She hung up the phone, sighed, and returned to the living room couch. Karen wrote a short note to slip under Mary's bedroom door telling her Sam would be downstairs. She left the bedroom and closed the door behind her.

***

Crocker had a new plan.

CHAPTER 22

When the jackhammer in my head and the flashes in my eyes subsided, I felt the cold concrete floor on my back. Soft light flooded the small corrugated iron shed through the clear PVC above.

I checked my pockets. No wallet, gun, or burner phone. They didn't find my cellphone strapped above my knee. My shirt pocket held a note. It was from Glick.

This is for the slashed tires. Stop looking for the girl or it'll be worse next time.

The good news was the headache meant I wasn't dead. The bad news was Glick had managed to slow me down. He was on my shit list, and I vowed to do something about it.

Rising slowly to my feet, my head tapped the roof. I waited for a wave of nausea to pass and then rattled the door and its frame, hearing a heavy padlock rock back and forth.

I squinted up at the roof in an effort to see while trying to block the light stabbing my eyes. Flat head roofing nails held it in place. The wind outside and occasional street traffic was all I could hear. I bent over, arced my arm, and rammed my fist into the corner of the roof. After slamming it five times, I pushed the loosened corner. Repeated pushing weakened two sides, and I could peek out.

There was a concrete wall with one boarded-up window and a door twenty feet away. A faded mural with red letters inside a blue oval read *'Esso.'* I could smell gasoline and see cars pulling in front.

More pushing and the roof opened enough for me to climb up, squeeze out, and tumble to the dry, dusty ground. I spotted an alley leading to a side street and took it. I remembered the wide street with seedy, rundown storefronts. At the end of the block, I could see the Gunslinger's Saloon. I ran in the opposite direction toward my rental truck.

The pickup was where I left it in the bank parking lot. I reached in the planter, retrieved the spare key, and drove past the Gunslinger Saloon looking for Glick or the locals who helped him. I doubted I'd see any of them in daylight and Glick was probably long gone. I needed luck if I was going to find my attackers and I wasn't having any. After an hour, I decided to head back to the hotel in Somerset.

***

I swallowed some ibuprofen and two cups of

coffee. After a hot shower, I gave Ray Scully a call.

"Twelfth, Scully here."

"Glad to see you on the day shift with the rest of the working stiffs."

"Holt, where are you? Did you wrap things up yet? I managed to choke down Regina's dry meatloaf last night by imagining the steak you promised. A double dose of mac and cheese helped too."

"I'm in Somerset, Pennsylvania. I'm still searching for the missing girl. Listen, I need another favor. Could you call the Stowe post office for me and find out the address in Broome, Pennsylvania where Martin's mail is forwarded?"

"Are you under the false impression I have nothing to do all day?" Scully asked. "And you still don't want to tell me what you're doing?"

"I'm looking for a seventeen-year-old girl."

"Hmm. I think in addition to the steak dinner, you have to buy me a couple of lap dances."

"Sure. Better take it easy with the mac and cheese or you won't have a lap. When's the last time you were at the gym?"

"When's the last time you got laid?"

I asked about Regina and the kids. I suppressed the thought of what I once had and lost, which clamored to escape the back of my mind where I keep it locked up.

***

It was late afternoon when Scully called and woke me from a nap.

"Ray, what've you got?"

"That address you need is twenty-six Adams Street. Hey, you don't sound so great."

"Just woke up, that's all. Listen, do you remember the name of Senator Grayson's lawyer? I think you interviewed him during the Rand investigation."

Scully was silent for a long moment.

"Why are you asking, Lucas? Does your case have anything to do with Grayson or the Rand case? If it does, you need to let me know. That case is still open, and if you have any new information, you need to tell me."

My head was foggy and I realized, too late, the mistake I'd made. "It has nothing to do with Rand's murder." It was close to the truth.

"Grayson is running for president, Holt. To start digging up the past for whatever reason will have the senator's people and brass all over us— especially me."

"I know. My client had a relationship with Grayson's lawyer, and I wanted his name, that's all. He may be able to help with my case."

"What kind of relationship? I'm getting a bad feeling, again."

"Forget it, Ray." I was about to disconnect.

"Wait." I could hear my friend's sigh of resignation. "His name is Douglas Cain."

"Thanks, appreciate it. I'll stay in touch."

"I'd rather you stay out of trouble."

CHAPTER 23

Karen and Mary crossed the trailhead to the entrance of Moose Horn Trail.

They had split the weight of what they carried between them. Used to camping, Karen held the two-person tent, her sleeping bag, and a backpack of water and snacks. Mary lugged her sleeping bag and a tote containing her I-Pod with a small separate speaker and extra clothes for both of them.

Karen, familiar with the terrain, deftly avoided ruts and uneven sections of the road. Mary looked in all directions as she kept up with the conversation and stepped in every pothole.

"Karen, Jason King wanted me to tell you he misses you in the stands at the baseball games."

"Yeah, well…I know what Jason misses." They both laughed for what seemed like the fiftieth time that day.

Karen thought about Jason. He was one of the reasons she didn't want to leave Stowe. They'd had a great time together going to baseball games, skiing, and hanging out with his friends. He never said it, but she knew he loved her and hoped for a future for both of them. Hugs, tears, and empty promises marked their last night alone. But now she was with Sam—at least until she went off to college.

Mary clicked her fingers in front of Karen. "Hello. Earth to Karen. Over."

"Sorry. I lost my mind for a moment. We go off this trail just a bit farther."

"No problem. I was doing some day dreaming too. My parents are talking about a trial separation. This is the first time I've been happy in weeks. Tonight we can forget all about parents and boyfriends."

Karen headed for the old campsite Sam had shown her. Accessed from a path a half mile along the main trail, the site had a lean-to half hidden by overgrown shrubs and clumps of tall birches. She thought about the last few times she'd been there with Sam and smiled.

"C'mon, Mary, let's move faster so we can set up before dark."

***

Crocker had returned to the barn, stashed his truck behind some brush, and then hiked back toward Moose Horn Trail along the unused path.

In place behind a clump of trees with a view of the main trail, he heard the girls' laughter and excited chatter. He looked through binoculars up toward the trail and saw his targets.

He followed off trail, navigating through thick

vegetation and over fallen, dead trees. His sweat attracted gnats and mosquitos that zeroed in on any warm-blooded mammal they could find.

Crocker was glad the girls kept up their conversation. Their voices carried and made tracking them easier. His attention perked up when he noticed the sudden quiet. He was too far below the trail to see them. He couldn't lose them—it would waste too much time to search for them in the dark.

He stopped dead when the ground crunched and someone spoke a few feet away from him. It was the girls; they had veered off the main road. As far as he knew, there was no public campsite there. He smirked. *My job just got easier.* Crocker continued to follow them through the woods.

***

"Almost there, Mary."

Five minutes later, they stepped into a clearing. A lean-to peeked out from under a pine tree in the center of twenty feet of dirt patches, leaves, and broken twigs. Early evening sun slanted through heavy branches to a circular stone fire pit Karen and Sam had built on their last visit.

Mary examined the lean-to. "It looks safe, I think." The only sound was a squirrel click-clicking up a tree. "I see why you and Sam come here. The other campsites are pretty far away."

Karen smiled at the implication. "No, that's why Sam comes here. I'm not ready for a serious relationship. Jason and I still keep in touch every week and…it's confusing." Karen stared at the ground, unsure of what she was feeling.

"C'mon, Karen. It's been a year. I'm not saying forget Jason. Just open yourself to other possibilities."

"Yes, well…Sam will be by later to make sure we are okay. Let's get the tent set up before we lose daylight."

***

Crocker tried to be patient.

The bugs, the slow crawl around trees through dense shrubs, and the damn waiting, wore him down and made him angry. Breathing deeply, he willed himself not to kill them both right there and then.

Assess the location, assess the target, move with purpose.

It was still light. He could see the girls from his position on the ground thirty yards away. He would have to bring the truck closer. They were far enough from other campsites not to see him, but not so far that they wouldn't hear the girls scream.

***

Karen gathered up kindling, placed it in the fire pit while Mary found dry, dead branches to place on top. The fire would provide light, warmth, and a cozy place to spend the evening.

"Mary, how about some music?"

"Sounds great. I'll get the iPod and speaker." A few minutes later, as the sun began to set, they listened to Arctic Monkeys sing "When the Sun Goes Down."

***

Crocker found a spot to park his black truck not far off Farm Road and hiked to their campsite. As he got closer, he dropped to the ground and crawled. He gashed his hands and face as he sluggishly slithered through the bushes. *What the hell kind of shrubs have thorns?* The sun's warm glow had turned to twilight. Dusk would soon follow. Crocker was close enough now to hear and see them, but not so close he risked discovery.

What was that noise? Crocker lay flat and froze. *Who the hell is that?* He saw the girls smile when a tall young man of about twenty approached.

This assignment is a nightmare.

***

Karen rose, hugged Sam, and introduced him to Mary.

"Hi, Mary," said Sam. "Karen has told me a lot about you."

"I've heard a bit about you too. This is a great camping spot. It's peaceful being this far from the other campers."

"Thanks. Two friends and I found it when we were hiking. There's room for three tents." Sam walked to the lean-to while talking, giving Mary the opportunity to mouth the words: *he's cute.* Time passed quickly as Karen and Mary told Sam stories of life in Stowe. Before Sam became too comfortable and decided to stay the night, Karen stood and said, "Okay, Sam. Mary and I are fine, and it's getting dark. Let me walk you back to the trail."

Sam made a lascivious grin at the offer. "Mary, have a great time. Watch out for the Ghost of Broome."

"What? If the ghost comes here, I'll kick his ass. Thanks for checking on us, Sam."

Sam took Karen's hand, and they headed toward the trail.

***

At last, I get a fuckin' break.

Crocker's eyes widened as his focus ramped up. He patted his shirt pocket, ensuring he had what he needed. He pulled his knees up to his chest and raised his head to peer over the shrubs. The other girl was sitting by the tent, raising the music volume. *Another break. She won't hear me comin'.* He didn't have much time.

Sacrificing stealth for a face pace, he moved one quick yard at a time. At the edge of the clearing, he knelt and listened for Karen returning. Nothing. Even the crickets were quiet.

Crocker parted the shrubs and stepped through. He cautiously padded toward Mary and pounced. He slapped his right hand over her mouth, sat on the ground, and wrapped both legs around her waist and arms to immobilize her. Her weak struggles served to wear her down. His left hand reached into his shirt pocket and took out a syringe.

He whispered, "Stop moving or die." She sat ramrod straight, held her breath and didn't move a muscle. Crocker put his thumb through the circle at the end of the plunger, pointed the syringe to the sky, and cleared the air bubble. He stabbed her arm through the light cotton fabric of her shirt as she again struggled, dislodging the syringe. *That should be enough.* Ten seconds later, her eyes shut. Her body relaxed and became dead weight.

***

"Stop it, Sam. You're acting like a damn octopus." Karen pushed away.

"Okay, okay. I just miss you."

She allowed Sam to keep his arms around her waist and hold her close. Karen needed to resolve her conflicted feelings toward him soon or she would drive him away. "I like you, Sam. I need more time to work things out. Now, go win a baseball game or something."

"Fine. Call if you need anything."

***

Crocker dragged Mary behind the shrubs.

Deciding he had a few moments before Karen returned, he stepped back into the campsite and shuffled his foot over the drag marks to erase them. With only a few seconds left, he ran to where Karen would enter the clearing and crouched behind a tree.

***

Karen meandered back to the campsite, thinking about a late snack. It was nearly dark, and she wondered if they had enough wood to keep the fire going all night. She broke through the clearing.

"Mary, do you think we need more wood?"

No answer.

"Mary?"

***

Crocker stepped out, placed his right hand around Karen's mouth...and received an ineffective elbow in the gut for his trouble. She grabbed the middle finger of his hand and pulled it away from her face. Crocker grunted. *Bitch.* He enclosed her arms with his left, and she stomped his foot hard. He needed to sedate her but was busy countering her blows. *Improvise.*

He drew his Glock and slammed the back of her head. Karen's body fell limp, and Crocker eased her to the ground. He took another syringe from his shirt pocket and plunged it into her arm.

After dropping Karen's body into the back of the truck, Crocker ran to the campsite to get Mary. Before retrieving his second victim, he paused, turning his attention to his surroundings. Faint music drifted from campsites off in the distance.

Crocker tore down the tent, wrapped it around one of the backpacks, and packed the tent poles. He stashed them in the shrubs behind the lean-to. He would come back later and scrub the area for evidence anyone had been there. He picked up the other backpack and trudged to where he'd left the girl. Stunned and swearing, he stared at the flattened patch of leaves and scrub where a body had previously lain.

Mary was gone.

He searched the area, frantic to find her before she would be able to alert anyone. Crocker sprinted toward the trail. A soft moaning stopped him in his tracks. He listened and then padded to a patch of junipers. Lying beneath them was Mary.

Her eyes widened at the sight of him and she opened her mouth to scream. Crocker dropped the backpack he held and lunged over her, clamping a hand over her mouth. His hand still in place, he rose, yanking her off the ground with his free arm. She kicked and bit him causing him to lose his grip. Unsteady from the partial dose Crocker had injected into her, Mary staggered a few feet and fell. *Fuck. I should have bashed this one on the head too.*

She rose, staggering to her feet as Crocker caught her by her shirt. It tore and she jerked free. Crocker was an arm's length away when Mary stumbled and fell, hitting her head against a rock.

He hoisted her onto his shoulder. She wouldn't give him any more trouble.

CHAPTER 24

The gilded Grand Ballroom at the Plaza Hotel pulsed with excitement. Two hundred supporters of Todd Grayson for President donated ten thousand dollars each to attend the gala.

Senator Grayson and his wife entered the room to thunderous applause. The senator escorted her to a seat at one of the gold linen-clad tables adorned with centerpieces of blue hydrangeas and white roses. A thirteen-piece orchestra played a medley from the American Songbook. Grayson took to the stage and gave a rousing speech, which earned him a standing ovation.

Todd Grayson rode high on vast approval in the polls. In his early fifties, physically attractive and with a velvet voice, he mesmerized people of both sexes. His moderate politics, at a time of unprecedented gridlock in Washington, appealed to voters on both sides of the political spectrum. As President, he vowed to lead an administration that would adapt to the current needs of the country rather than adhere to staunch party ideologies.

At the end of his well-received discourse, Grayson signaled for the orchestra to resume playing and stepped down from the stage. On the way to his table, supporters stopped him to shake his hand to express their delight and what a privilege it was to attend such an event. The senator thanked them one by one, catching his wife's eye as he neared. He winked.

Maeve Grayson, petite and regal in orchid silk chiffon that complemented her porcelain complexion and dark hair, waved to her husband. She turned to speak to a woman who approached her. The senator beamed with pride for the smart and elegant lady he married—who would be a magnificent First Lady.

About to join his wife, Senator Todd Grayson froze.

He recognized the tall, blonde woman to whom his wife spoke. His warm smile turned to a stiffened grin, and with ice in his veins, he continued forward to stand next to Maeve. She slipped her arm around one of his, drawing him closer.

"Todd, I'd like you to meet Janet Maxwell. Her late husband was president of Maxwell Investments. Mrs. Maxwell has graciously donated on his behalf, as he was a fervent supporter."

Grayson extended his hand for a formal shake. "Thank you so much, Mrs. Maxwell. I knew your husband and was very sorry to hear of his passing— and your son's. Such a tragedy."

Janet Maxwell held onto the senator's hand longer than necessary, her azure eyes daring him to acknowledge a past acquaintance.

"Thank you for your condolences. I find I can bear the loss much better if I'm busy and involved in some of my husband's past endeavors. One of those being your pursuit of the presidency."

Maeve Grayson let go of her husband's arm. "If you'll excuse me, darling, I want to say hello to Ann and David Walsh. So nice to have met you, Mrs. Maxwell."

"Please call me Janet. It was lovely to meet you too. I hope we will see more of each other during the course of the campaign. I plan to support the senator in any way I can."

As Janet watched Mrs. Grayson cross to the other side of the room to greet her friends, Todd Grayson's gaze swept over the woman from his past. He hadn't seen her in nearly eighteen years. He would have liked to say he hadn't thought of her, but that would be a lie.

Grayson met twenty-four-year-old Janet Coughlin at a DC fundraiser for a non-profit organization for whom she worked. He always had a roving eye, and this young woman caught his attention with her energy as well as her beauty. A political science major, with a minor in business, Janet shared many of his ideals and his vision for their great country. Her vivacious nature and ingenuity, which stimulated his mind, also extended to the bedroom. He thought if he hadn't already been married, he might have fallen in love with her. Perhaps he had.

Their affair lasted a year. He moved his family to a suburb outside the beltway and rented an apartment in New York City for when he had business there. Janet left DC and took a job on Wall Street at an investment firm. She lived in the city, not far from the senator.

Grayson's presidential aspirations germinated early in his career. His path was clear. When Janet told him she was pregnant, he panicked, ended the relationship, and sent Cain to deal with the situation. Grayson only saw her once after the breakup. She conned her way into his apartment so she could slap his face and return some jewelry he'd given her. Janet never cried or made a scene. She never begged him to leave his wife and be a father to her child. He thought it strange. It was as if she expected he would make the right decision on his own, and God help him if he didn't.

An awkward silence passed as Grayson thought how to begin a conversation with a woman he knew must hate him. *What do I say? Long time, no see. Hey, you look great. Why the hell are you here?* He almost said the last aloud when she spoke.

"For a man who believes he has what it takes to lead the free world, you look positively terrified, Todd."

She leaned toward him, almost cheek to cheek. "And you should be. You have that 'caught with your hand in the cookie jar' look. Your wife is lovely, by the way. She adores you, I can tell. But she doesn't know you like I do."

Every muscle in Grayson's body balled into a knot. Only she could get away with speaking to him that way. Not even Maeve would dare point out his weaknesses. He willed himself not to show his discomfort and hoped he wouldn't choke on his words. He took a subtle deep breath.

"What should I be afraid of? Whatever game you're playing, you should consider your chances of winning."

He knew better than to spar with her, but he couldn't help it. A server with a tray of filled fluted glasses stopped in front of them and offered champagne. They both accepted the drink. She was as adept as he was at presenting a cool exterior. If one didn't know better, it would appear they were discussing the wonderful music. Janet sipped the bubbly and then turned to Grayson and smiled.

"Is that what it was to you? A game? Do you think it's over and you've won?"

Grayson gripped the glass in his palm. *Don't respond. Let it go. She's baiting you.* Not heeding his own advice, the words spilled from his mouth.

"What do you want, Janet? What could you possibly want after all this time?"

"Time heals all wounds. Is that what you think, Todd?"

"I think enough time has passed where we can both accept the choices we made."

"You mean the ones you made for yourself and for me?"

"What are you going to do? Tell me."

Janet finished her champagne as another server walked by. She deposited the glass on the tray. A gentleman came toward them. Janet waved to him and then cocked her head back at Grayson and raised a brow.

"Now, that would spoil the surprise, wouldn't it?"

Cain had assured him he had taken care of everything—assured him Janet had moved on when she married a Wall Street trader who started his own investment firm. She'd had a son and until six weeks before, Janet Maxwell was happy in her life and out of his.

Now she was back—and he feared with a vengeance.

CHAPTER 25

"Todd."

He heard his name and blinked. Janet Maxwell was no longer at his side. Maeve had finished speaking to the Walshes and moved on to...*What's his name?* He knew the man; it was right on the tip of his tongue. *Damn.* He saw Janet in her blue gown weave through the crowd toward his wife.

A hand touched his back. "Todd, are you all right?"

Grayson kept his eyes on Janet. "Cain, this is your fault."

"Todd, I'm doing everything I can, but you know what she's like. We have to tread very carefully."

The senator spoke through a practiced smile he hoped would disguise the fact his gut churned and his mind swam with thoughts of the havoc Maxwell could wreak on his life.

"I told you I want the problem resolved—gone."

Cain moved closer, his mouth at the senator's ear. "Be reasonable, Todd. What do you want me to do, arrange an accident?"

Todd Grayson turned to look at his lawyer, his face taut, his gray eyes steeled with anger. "Don't *ever* talk like that to me in public again. How you do your job is your concern. My only concern is that you do it."

"Douglas, how are you?" Maeve Grayson interrupted the tense moment, extending two arms as she moved toward Cain for a kiss on both cheeks. "You and Roberta should have dinner with us sometime."

Cain spent a few minutes engaging in small talk with Mrs. Grayson before he left her and the senator to go back to his table. The wait staff laid a salad of fresh mixed greens and colorful vegetables at each place setting. Guests filled the dance floor, not appearing anxious to sit down to a meal.

"Todd, let's dance." Maeve took her husband's hand and led him to the parquet floor. He let her guide him, his attention still on the blue-gowned woman. "You seem lost, dear. Something wrong?"

Grayson broke his surveillance and looked down at Maeve. "How could I be lost when I have you?" He leaned down and kissed her. She smiled and rested her head on his shoulder. As the orchestra played, a female singer performed a rendition of Celine Dion's "It's All Coming Back to Me."

He stiffened when Janet Maxwell and her dance partner moved into his space. She did not look at him, her attention on the gentleman. Despite the vehemence her presence conjured, he could not stop looking at her. She was a distraction he couldn't afford. Striking in her ice-blue evening dress, Maxwell had removed the satin shawl to reveal a plunging neckline, which drew Grayson's stare. Like it or not, it was all coming back to him.

Maeve's hand touched his cheek, forcing him to turn away but not before he noticed the jewel Janet Maxwell wore around her neck. Its familiarity chilled him to the bone.

CHAPTER 26

The town of Broome, Pennsylvania stood quaint and quiet in the southeastern part of the keystone state. At last count, population hovered at just over three hundred. Settled in the early eighteen hundreds around two churches built at opposite ends of the main street, the town lay in a valley on the Yough River.

Most of the residents of Broome were direct descendants of the first settlers. The rest were considered outsiders no matter how many decades they lived there. Half the adults worked outside the town and the other half maintained the school, the businesses, and the church ministries. The one doctor, Alex Clancy, was also the medical examiner. Law enforcement consisted of a sheriff and chief deputy.

The loud pounding on the front door of her tiny shed-roofed house roused Sheriff Madeline Grange from a sound sleep. She glanced outside at the darkness, picked up her cellphone, and noticed the missed call. *Damn it.*

Maddie grabbed a robe, combed splayed fingers through her wild red hair and yanked open the door. She glared at the tall, lanky man who'd disturbed the first decent two hours of sleep she'd had in a week.

"This better be good, Brimmer."

Deputy Chief Steve Brimmer's eyes roamed over the disheveled woman. Five foot ten and built in a way men find pleasing, he'd only seen her preened, with her gorgeous hair pulled back in a chignon. His mouth slack, the deputy stood still and silent.

"Brimmer." Maddie snapped her fingers in front of his face.

"Oh, yeah." He shook off the trance. "Someone found a body."

***

Sheriff Grange, dressed in her uniform of slacks, shirt, and ankle boots, strode a quarter of a mile along the trail. She stopped at a break in the tree line that wouldn't be noticeable if you weren't looking for it. The sheriff treaded the narrow path down an incline to where Dr. Alex Clancy knelt next to the body.

"Alex, have we got an identification and cause of death?"

"No ID. All I can tell you for sure is the victim is female Caucasian between fifteen and twenty-one. As you can see, the body has already started to decompose. Probably due to the warm temperatures and the fact it was partially submerged in water."

Deputy Brimmer trudged over to Maddie.

"Sheriff, I checked the area, but so far I don't see any personal effects. I did notice some fresh breaks in the vegetation along the path we took to get down here."

"You're saying she rolled or was rolled down the incline to land in this spot?"

Steve Brimmer nodded. "Looks that way to me."

"Great, so we've trampled all over possible evidence. Check areas along the trail for any sign of where she was walking or carried from."

Alex Clancy looked up from the body. "She has what appears to be a blow to the back of her head. She was either hit or fell on something."

Sheriff Grange turned to Brimmer. "Then we should check the area for blood. Maybe a stone or large rock."

"That's a lot of ground to cover for the two of us, Sheriff."

"Yeah, I'll call in some of our auxiliary reserve to help. Make sure we have enough gloves and evidence bags to go around."

Maddie made a phone call to Peter Delaney, who alerted the other trained reserve deputies. Most of them were local business owners able to take time to assist the sheriff. She returned to the medical examiner.

"How long do you think she's been there, Alex?"

"I'd say eight to twelve hours."

"I wonder if she was alone out here. What do you think?"

"Not my area to wonder, Sheriff. I deal with facts."

Sheriff Grange scanned the length of the body.

"Any signs of a struggle?"

Dr. Clancy glanced up toward the trail. "When McIntyre and a few others get here, they can help get the body bagged. I'll know more when I get her over to the morgue."

"You mean that nice sterile room you've got tucked away at the back of your house? How do you live there?"

Clancy rose from the ground. He stood eye to eye with the sheriff and smiled. "They're corpses, Maddie, not zombies."

Sheriff Grange left Clancy to deal with the body and found Deputy Brimmer on the trail talking to a small group of onlookers who had gathered.

"Folks, we're in the middle of an investigation and you must leave the area. The trail is closed until further notice."

"Sheriff!" one in the group shouted. "Who is it?"

"Male or female?" another asked. "Was it murder?"

The crowd fell silent at that—murder was nigh on unheard of in Broome. Maddie recognized Sam Gentry, whom she knew had five daughters ranging in age from twelve to twenty-five.

"Sam, are all your girls present and accounted for?"

"Yes, Sheriff. Are you saying it's a young girl?"

"I'm not saying anything, Sam. We can't answer any questions until we know more. You all go on home now and let us do our jobs."

Maddie signaled to Jim Simmons, one of the reserve deputies. "Please escort this group back to the main road."

She turned to Brimmer. "Steve, I want the area at the main road cordoned off with tape. That should have been done first thing. Tell Simmons to stay down there and keep anyone else from entering this trail. And get me some coffee."

***

The morning sun broke through the clusters of beeches and yellow birch, eliminating the need for spotlights. The volunteer crew packed up the equipment and scoured the immediate grounds for blood and trace evidence, a nearly impossible job in thick undergrowth.

Maddie Grange watched from the edge of the trail as the reserves canvassed a fifty-yard radius from where the body had lain. Steve Brimmer, back from barricading the entrance to the trail, carried two containers of coffee. He held out one to Maddie. "Light and sweet."

"Thanks, Steve." Maddie sipped the hot beverage. "Hmm, this is a good start. I'm going to need at least a gallon more to get through this day."

"Doc Clancy said he'll get started on the preliminaries to ascertain cause of death."

The sheriff nodded. "I'd like to be able to identify her as soon as possible."

"Well, news of the discovery is spreading like wildfire. I imagine someone will come forward with some information. Everybody knows everything that goes on in this town."

"That's what I thought, but the victim could be an outsider." Sheriff Grange took a large gulp of her drink. "I'm heading back to the office. Keep me posted."

Maddie returned to the trailhead where she had parked her car. Moose Horn was a popular walking and biking trail during the summer months. Broome counted on the tourist trade from an influx of hikers. They were enamored with the town's quaint main street and shops adorned with flowerboxes and pots of vibrant summer blooms. The sheriff groaned in anticipation of the Mayor's reaction to a possible homicide discouraging summer trade. Her cellphone rang.

"Sheriff Grange."

"Maddie, it's me."

She recognized Clancy's voice. "You have something already?"

"In addition to a subdural hematoma, there are bruises on her arms and wrists. This is just a preliminary, but it looks like she may have struggled with someone. I'd say she was pushed or restrained in some way and fell after freeing herself."

"You're saying, either way, another person was involved."

"That's how it appears."

"Thanks, Alex."

Maddie closed her eyes and sighed. *I was really hoping it was an accident.* She reached her late model Ford Explorer, slid in behind the wheel, and started the truck. Backing out of a parking space, she glanced in her rearview and slammed on the brakes.

Steve Brimmer ran from the trail, shouting her

name and waving one arm for her to stop the car. The sheriff rolled down her window.

"Sheriff, Sheriff! We found something." Brimmer held up a teal blue backpack, caked with mud and leaves. "We found this bag and think it belonged to the victim. There's an ID." He handed her a small quilted, floral card case, a plastic cover protecting the driver's license it held. The photo was of a young woman. The date of birth put her age at seventeen.

Her name was Karen Martin.

CHAPTER 27

What a difference a half hour makes. Where Smoulder exemplified decay and decline, Broome bristled with life and exuberance.

People crowded the tree-lined main street, shopping, strolling, or eating outside the few restaurants and cafes. I drove straight through the town. Gypsy indicated I make a right turn before Moose Horn Trailhead on Castle Road and another on Adams Street. A group of hikers, who I recognized by their attire and walking sticks, engaged in animated conversation with the local law enforcement. Yellow tape blocked the entrance to the trail.

I continued to Adams, found number twenty-six, and parked across the street. The Martin's small gray saltbox backed up to woods. Red maples shaded the front and sides. The nearest house stood a half a block away. One car sat in the driveway—a red sedan, which looked to be about fifteen years old. The house appeared quiet. It had rained the night before and the driveway was still damp except for a bone-dry section under the car. Either someone was still home or they left to go somewhere on foot.

Still on my guard after my run in with Glick and company, I climbed two steps to the front door and rang the bell. I heard the chime and waited a full minute before I rang it again. Turning from the door, I noticed fuzzy red and white dice hanging from the rearview mirror of the car. I walked over to take a closer look. A Temple University cap lay on the shelf behind the back seat. Half-empty bottles of water sat on the passenger front seat and a balled-up pink sweatshirt on the center console. I surmised the car belonged to Karen Martin.

Since no one appeared to be home, I walked the half block to a neighbor and rang the bell. A woman immediately yanked open the door, giving me the impression she'd been standing on the other side waiting for someone to call. At a guess, I'd say she was about seventy and dressed in a voluminous muumuu. She eyed me from behind thick white-rimmed glasses. I pulled out my ID.

"Hello, I'm Lucas Holt. I wonder if you could help me. I'm looking for the Martins. Karen in particular."

I took a step back when she pushed past me to go outside. She craned her head and looked toward the Martin house.

"Car's in the driveway. Why don't you ring their bell?"

"I did that, ma'am. No one is answering. Do you know the Martins?"

"Sure, I know everybody, though I don't make it

157

my business to know everything they do. I'm not a busybody."

"Of course not." I showed her the picture Barbara Hansen gave me. "Is this Karen?"

"Yes, it is. That looks like Overlook Rock she's sitting on. Can't see it in the picture, but there's a nice view of a ravine along the trail."

"So she likes to hike."

"Sure, lots of folks here do. If she's not home, maybe she's gone hiking."

"What about her parents? Do they work? I realize its Sunday, perhaps they work weekends too."

"Don't know about that. It's Sunday already? Goodness, seems like it was just yesterday when I went to church. I'd better go. Have to do my hair."

Without another word, she turned and went inside, shutting the door behind her.

I drove back into the town and found a spot near one of the cafes.

Settling into a seat outside, I scanned the menu and ordered a grilled chicken sandwich and an iced tea. No beer as my head was still a bit foggy. I wore a ball cap and sunglasses, first to keep the sun from adding to my pulsing headache, and second so people wouldn't know I was looking at them. Facing the street, I kept an eye out for Glick. If he'd come as far as Smoulder, chances were he knew the Martins lived in Broome—and that meant whomever he worked for knew it too.

The waitress brought my sandwich and drink. The nausea that accompanied the knob on my head passed. Not realizing how hungry I was, I ate like I was going to the chair.

A man walked up to the table of diners next to mine and mumbled something I couldn't hear. The reaction from those seated was immediate—they all looked stunned. "A dead body?" "Oh my God, where?" "An accident, I'm sure."

They all talked at once until the bearer of the bad news said, "I hear they think she was murdered."

The skin at my neck prickled and a shiver spread through my body. *What are the chances?* Again, I thought, what lengths would someone go to stop me from finding Karen Martin? I paid the check and drove to the trailhead—I knew the reason for the yellow tape.

***

I spotted a man with a Sheriff's badge, who turned out to be Chief Deputy Steve Brimmer.

Sidling through the crowd still gathered at the trail entrance, I stood next to the deputy with my ID ready to show. After telling everyone they needed to move on, he made a half turn and almost walked into me. Startled, he pulled up short, tipped his hat back, and looked up at me. I removed my cap and sunglasses. He waved me away.

"Sir, excuse me, we need to clear this area. We have a crime scene up the road."

"Yes, I see that." I held out my PI license. "I'm looking for a young woman, seventeen years of age. Her name is Karen Martin."

Chief Deputy Brimmer narrowed his eyes.

"You need to see the sheriff."

"Can you direct me to him?"

"Her. Sheriff Grange is a woman." Brimmer scanned the parking lot. "That your Rover?"

I grinned, thinking I must've stuck out like a sore thumb in my pressed jeans and my Salvatore Ferragamo loafers. I thought the t-shirt and cap made up for them.

"Yes." I nodded at the car marked "Sheriff." "Shall I follow you?"

He looked at his car, at my Rover and then at me.

"I'll ride with you. One minute."

Brimmer gave me his back and pulled out his phone. I assumed he called the sheriff to give her a heads up.

"Let's go." He extended his arm. I strode toward the SUV and Brimmer followed.

***

The Broome Sheriff's Office occupied another saltbox-style building. I parked in one of the designated spots in front and entered after the deputy. A reception desk and chairs constituted a waiting area. Through an iron-gated doorway behind the desk, I could see a couple of holding cells. Brimmer pointed to a staircase. The sheriff was upstairs.

Two desks, occupied by a young man and a woman, stood to one side of an open space at the top. A seating area lay on the other. Beyond the seats were two glass-fronted offices. We passed an empty office, which the name on the door indicated belonged to Deputy Brimmer. In the other, a woman with deep red hair pulled back from her face sat at her desk immersed in some reading. Brimmer held his arm out and told me to wait. She looked up when the deputy knocked on the door, entered, and closed it behind him.

Sheriff Grange glanced back and forth from Brimmer to me as the deputy spoke. When done, he turned to open the door. I could feel the Sheriff's suspicious glare, which did not alter even after the introduction.

"Sheriff Grange, this is Lucas Holt, a PI from New York—or so his ID says. He's looking for Karen Martin."

I wasn't sure why he repeated what he had undoubtedly told the Sheriff, but her eyes widened as if she heard it for the first time. She rose from her seat, tall and formidable, and stretched out her hand.

"Mr. Holt. I'm Madeline Grange. Have a seat."

I sat. She remained standing for a few minutes, while Steve Brimmer filled her in on how he had managed to clear the trailhead of spectators. I used the time to assess Madeline Grange and couldn't help noticing her well-formed figure. Dressed conservatively in law-enforcement tan slacks, belted at her slim waist, and shirt tucked and buttoned to her long neck, she exuded authority. At least that's what I told myself she was exuding. The update over, the sheriff sat down. Deputy Brimmer nodded to me on his way out.

Sheriff Grange resumed her glare and asked to see my ID. I obliged. She didn't hand it back before she spoke.

"Mr. Holt, why are you looking for Karen

Martin?"

I had to think twice about giving an agent of the law the white lie concerning an inheritance. "Karen Martin is adopted and her birth mother is trying to locate her."

"What do you know about her?"

"Not much, I'm afraid. The Martins lived in Vermont before they moved here. Karen is seventeen—she holds a Vermont driver's license. Her father was a ski instructor in Vermont. Her mother was a homemaker."

"I imagine the adoption was closed and the birth mother doesn't know who the adoptive parents are or where they live. What led you to Broome?"

"The adoption was closed in that my client didn't know where the child was or have any part in her upbringing. But as part of the arrangement, she received updates about her daughter and a photo now and then."

"Unusual arrangement." Madeline Grange relaxed back in her chair, hands in her lap, still holding my ID.

"Yes. In any case, she stopped receiving updates two years ago. She's lost her own family in an accident and is anxious to find her only living biological child."

"While that's a sad story, you realize the young woman you seek is still a minor. Even if I had any information on her whereabouts, I couldn't tell you."

"I traced her to a home on Adams Street. A neighbor confirmed she lives there. No one seems to be home."

Sheriff Grange sat straight up. "She lives in Broome?"

"Yes, twenty-six Adams Street."

The sheriff stood and left her office. I followed to the doorway.

"Steve, take a couple of the reserves and check out twenty-six Adams. Mr. Holt says Karen Martin lives there."

Deputy Brimmer nodded. "Sure thing. I hate having to deliver bad news."

"Steve, we don't have a positive ID yet."

"Right, sorry, Maddie." Brimmer spoke to the sheriff, but his eyes were on me.

Madeline Grange turned. "Mr. Holt, I'm sorry I can't discuss Karen Martin. This is an ongoing investigation."

"An investigation into what?"

"Into the death of a young woman found near Moose Horn Trail. That's all I can say."

Sheriff Grange rushed past me. I inhaled the fresh earthy scent of woods and citrus. I called to her with a little more strain in my voice than I intended.

"Sheriff."

Madeline Grange twisted her head toward me.

"Really, Mr. Holt, I'm very busy."

"Just one more thing."

Her shoulders shrank with exasperation, and she pushed one errant strand of hair off her face. "What is it?"

I smiled and pointed to the hand at her side still clutching my ID.

"Could I have my wallet back?"

Chapter 28

Left standing alone in the sheriff's office, I recapped the information gleaned from meeting Sheriff Grange. I knew there was a strong possibility the dead girl was Karen Martin. A possibility because the body hadn't been positively identified. The sheriff would need to locate the Martins for that. I wondered where they were. Had something happened to them too? My job was to find Karen. Alive. I dreaded having to tell Janet Maxwell her daughter was dead, and I hadn't planned to investigate her death. Before I got too ahead of myself, I needed to get all the facts.

Outside on the street, I noticed the cluster of people had turned away from the trailhead and gravitated to the sheriff's office. Murder in Broome would be the main event for a long time. I meandered through the crowd, picking out a gentleman in tan chinos, oxford shirt, and a straw fedora. He looked like a professor on summer break. I moved next to him and started a conversation.

"Morning. Terrible what happened, eh?"

Professor, who wore metal-framed glasses, smoothed his short gray mustache with his fingers, and nodded.

"Terrible. Puts a real damper on things. Hope they find out what happened soon."

He looked me over but didn't ask who I was. Instead, I questioned him.

"Do you live in Broome?"

"Yes, I do. Forty years. Don't recall any murders."

"I don't believe the sheriff has ruled it a murder yet."

"True enough. Rumors are flying, though. Heard from the wife of a deputy, who brought the body over to Dr. Clancy's morgue, there was evidence of a struggle."

"Where is the morgue?"

"Doc Clancy lives over on Chambers. Biggest house in Broome. Sits on a hill—can't miss it. Clancys were a family of morticians here for a long time. It used to be a mortuary. Until Alex became a doctor. Now it's the medical examiner's office."

I was about to drive to Chambers when a sheriff's car plowed down the street, honking for the crowd to get out of the way. I could see Deputy Brimmer at the wheel. Two people sat in the back. He turned into a parking spot, and exited the car.

Another car pulled next to him. Four men, who I surmised were deputized assistants, jumped out and took over crowd control. Brimmer opened a backseat door and extended his arm to help an attractive, petite woman out of the sheriff's car. A man slipped out the other side. Tall, with dark brown hair, flecked with gray, and a trim, athletic build, he walked around the car and took hold of the woman's arm. I could see the grave look on their faces.

They had to be Daniel and Sarah Martin.

***

Knowing police procedures when it came to dead bodies, I decided to drive over to Chambers. I didn't know the particulars, such as how long the body lay in the woods or the condition of the corpse. But physical identification by next of kin is the fastest way to prove identity. It wouldn't be long before the sheriff escorted the Martins to the medical examiner's office. It was an overwhelming and dreadful task, but necessary. I sympathized with the Martins.

Chambers, a wide, tree-lined street, intersected the main street in the middle of Broome's busy town square. The road veered from the public area and wound up a hill, populated with thick woodlands, to a lone structure. A large clapboard and stone house, in mild disrepair, stood at the top. The ornate roof, with what I believe architects call a widows walk, gave it a haunted house appearance—apropos for a mortuary…or morgue.

I passed the house, turned around, and parked under a large maple. My position afforded shade and a good vantage point to see who came and went. While I waited, I pulled out the Rand file and scanned the crime scene photos. I remembered thinking at the time something wasn't right. The way she died and the physical evidence didn't ring completely true with a crime of passion—which is what Scully and I thought it was.

Sheila Rand died from a fatal stab wound to the stomach, but we never found the murder weapon. Since we couldn't ascertain if anything was missing from the victim's home, we assumed the perpetrator either took the weapon with him or brought his own.

Rand's evening occupation, her attendance at political soirees, and the eyewitness report, all pointed to Grayson or someone of his ilk. Hence, we settled on passion. I honestly couldn't see Grayson planning and executing a murder. If it was premeditated, he would have had someone else do it—and in a much more professional manner. This murder was sloppy.

Well, sloppy in its execution—the fact they got away with it, in my opinion, was sheer luck. Shuffling through the photos, I paused at the close-up of Rand's head and torso. There were multiple wounds on her chest, arms, and, of course, the one big hole in her stomach. Except for a small cut on Rand's chin and another on one ear, her face had been untouched by the knife. The defensive wounds on her arms could have been due to the killer's attempt to slash his victim's face as well. The missing hair would indicate the assailant, who was taller than Rand, had grabbed a clump of hair to hold the head steady. I laid the file aside when a car rose over the hill.

As expected, the sheriff's car pulled in front of

Dr. Clancy's home. Brimmer emerged from the driver's seat and glanced to where I was parked. He didn't appear to recognize my Rover or he had other things on his mind. Sheriff Grange exited the passenger side. She looked my way too and paused. I could almost feel that same steady glare she had leveled at me in her office.

Madeline Grange, as far as I knew, didn't know the type of vehicle I drove. She turned away and spoke to Brimmer who looked once again in my direction. This time I detected a frown on the officer's face.

The thought I'd irritated the sheriff in some way made me chuckle. I watched as she led Daniel and Sarah Martin up the stone steps toward the house where they would be asked to identify the body.

A smirk left my face, replaced by anger when someone pounded on my car window. So intent on Sheriff Grange's movements, I hadn't seen Brimmer come up beside my vehicle. I rolled down the window.

"Take it easy there, chief, these windows are expensive to replace."

"Yeah, like that's a concern of yours." Brimmer's frown revealed the lack of a sense of humor and a mild dislike for a PI from the Big Apple. I remained silent and waited for him to tell me my offense.

"You can't park here. Move on, Mr. Holt."

"Really? I don't see any signs to that effect."

"It's an unwritten law. There's no loitering on our streets."

"Parking your car is loitering?"

"Parking and just sitting in it is." Brimmer clenched his jaw and kept glancing between Dr. Clancy's house and me. The deputy appeared anxious to go inside to where events more important than my loitering were unfolding.

I thought I had tortured Brimmer long enough. I'd swing back later and speak to the medical examiner. I wanted to get another look at the Martins. Daniel Martin at least fit the physical description of a ski instructor—unlike his imposter. I hoped to speak with them at some point. Before I could relieve the suffering deputy of his painful duty by pulling away, Sheriff Grange and the Martins came out of the house. And looked less distraught than I'd have expected.

Brimmer noticed too. "That's strange. Holt, move the car. I've got to go." The deputy took off toward Grange and the Martins. After some brief words, they piled into the car. Sheriff Grange hesitated before sinking down to the front passenger seat, looked in my direction, and shook her head no.

CHAPTER 29

Following the sheriff's car to see where they brought the Martins was my first choice, but I didn't want to push my luck. After Sheriff Grange so graciously indicated the body in the morgue was not Karen Martin, I owed her some space. She was back to square one. We both were.

I still had to locate Karen Martin.

Enough time had passed for the sheriff to bring the Martins back to her office or to drop them at home. My guess was they were home. I also had every reason to believe there would be a couple of sheriff's deputies keeping them company.

I drove to Adams Street. To my surprise, the only other car besides the red sedan was another red sedan in the driveway. A late model Toyota with Pennsylvania plates.

Striding up the walk, I noticed someone pull aside a window curtain and let it drop. The front door swung open and Daniel Martin stepped out. He met me halfway. His hair was a mess, his face lined with worry, and his eyes glossed with unshed tears.

He must have assumed I was one of the reserve deputies, there to give him news.

"Did you find her?"

"I'm sorry—"

"Oh God, no!"

I had to catch him before he sunk to the ground.

"No, no, Mr. Martin. I'm not here about your daughter."

Daniel Martin's eyes bore into me, and I could feel the heat of his anger at the misrepresentation of my presence at his house.

"I mean, I am here about Karen. But I'm not here to tell you anything has happened to her. I'm not with the sheriff's office."

He yanked his arms free, raked his fingers through his hair, and straightened to his full height.

"So, who the hell are you, and what do you want?"

"My name is Lucas Holt." I pulled out my ID. "I've been hired to find your daughter."

"A PI? I don't understand. Who hired you?"

"Mr. Martin, perhaps I could come inside and speak with you and your wife."

Daniel Martin didn't respond. He turned and walked back to his house. I followed hoping he wouldn't slam the door in my face. He didn't, leaving it wide open for me to enter. I stepped into the living room and closed the door behind me.

You could tell a lot about people by the way they lived. The tidy room and its overstuffed furniture evoked a comfortable order. Shoes lined up like soldiers on a mat by the door. Magazines stacked neatly under a side table. Shelves held books, arranged according to height. Framed photos crowded together on the white fireplace mantle, a console table, and an upright piano—all were of the same girl at various stages of life. The Martins enjoyed an organized life and Karen was at the center.

A woman sat on the sofa. She looked as harried as her husband did. I pushed aside memories of my own torment, a skill I'd honed since my investigative work focused almost exclusively on missing children or kidnapped victims.

"Sarah, this is Mr. Holt. He's a private investigator. He says he's been hired to find Karen."

Mrs. Martin gave me a questioning look. Daniel Martin sat next to his wife and pointed to a chair. I sat down.

"Mr. and Mrs. Martin, you've had a very trying day. Am I to understand the body you viewed at the morgue was not Karen?" I looked at Sarah Martin. "I'm sorry you had to go through the process."

"My wife didn't see the body," Daniel said.

"No?"

"Doctor Clancy told us there was some decomposition so it might be difficult. He asked us if Karen had any distinguishing physical traits. In fact, she has a small strawberry birthmark on her lower back."

I thought it was clever and considerate of the medical examiner to find a way to spare the Martins. Although many parents and next of kin find it necessary to see for themselves, a decomposed corpse vaguely resembles the person who lived.

"I'm glad it wasn't your daughter."

"Yes, you can't imagine how relieved we were," Sarah said. "But, Doctor Clancy then asked Daniel if he would be able to identify her. Karen's friend Mary was to visit."

"Were you able to make an identification?" I asked Daniel Martin.

"Yes..." Martin paused and rubbed his eyes with the back of his fisted right hand. "Yes, it's Mary Wells. We're heartbroken for the parents. Sheriff Grange is trying to contact them."

"We still don't..." Sarah Martin's words caught in her throat and she began to cry. Daniel finished for her.

"We don't know where Karen is. Sarah and I went away for a few days. Karen said she and Mary would spend the time together, catching up. Mary's parents were traveling to Ohio and planned to drop her off here."

"And did you speak to Karen while you were away? Did they tell you their plans?"

"She sent us a text after Mary arrived to say everything was fine and they were going to hike the trail and probably camp out."

"Camp out? The two girls by themselves?"

"Oh yes," Sarah said. "Many young people in Broome hike and camp out together. She's done it before. There are designated campsites. The Sheriff's office is very good about checking up on them."

"Did you give Sheriff Grange this information?"

Daniel Martin nodded. "Yes, we did. She said they already cleared the campgrounds and if Karen and her friend were among them, they'd be back in town. But you never know. Some teens have been known to wander into deeper woods to make camp."

"When was the last time you spoke to Karen?"

Sarah hesitated. "We haven't spoken to her since we left for Virginia. You know kids. All they want to do is text."

"When was the last text?"

Sarah twisted her hands together. "The day they went camping—in the morning. We didn't hear from her that night and figured the girls were busy enjoying each other's company. Then we fell asleep, and when I tried to text and then call the next day, there was no answer."

Daniel Martin spoke. "We intended to stay a few more days with my wife's brother, but came back so we could make sure everything was all right."

"But it wasn't." Sarah Martin's voice shook. "Oh God, we have to find her."

Before they succumbed to their panic, I wanted to make it clear I was there to help find Karen.

"I can help you, but I need to ask you a few more questions."

Sarah wept against her husband's shoulder. He held her tight.

"Yes," he said. "Anything you want to know."

I gave the Martins a few minutes to compose themselves. I was sure they were mentally chastising themselves for not keeping in better touch with their daughter. Granted, Karen was almost eighteen years old, but children are never too old to keep tabs on—even grown children. In this age of cellphones, the young tend to prefer communicating via text messages than with phone calls. I'm old fashioned. I like to hear the person I'm conversing with—besides, I can't type worth a damn.

Sarah Martin made coffee. It was good and strong. I had a feeling after my conversation with the Martins that I would be up for a while.

"I understand your daughter is adopted."

Sarah Martin took her husband's hand and squeezed. She nodded.

"Yes."

Daniel Martin eyed me with suspicion.

"Who hired you, Mr. Holt?"

Since Karen would reach the age of majority within the year, she could decide to reunite with her mother if she chose. It was best to be honest with the Martins.

"Her birth mother."

If the Martins appeared worried before, they looked terrified after I told them who hired me.

Daniel Martin shook his head in disbelief. "That's impossible."

"Why do you say that?" I asked. "It's highly probable that in many adoptions birth parents and children will opt to search for each other. Does Karen know she's adopted?"

Both Martins averted their eyes from me. Sarah glanced around the room. Tears slipped down her face. Daniel closed his, took a deep breath, and looked at me.

"No. She doesn't know."

Before I could say anything, Sarah spoke. "It

wasn't up to us. We were told not to tell her. We were told neither parent wanted to know her. Ever."

I could absolutely believe Senator Grayson would not want the little matter of an illegitimate love child getting in the way of his rise to the presidency. But from what Janet Maxwell told me, she had hoped to find a way to raise the child herself if she could. I remembered Maxwell's mood shifts during our meeting at McAllister's.

"Thank you for speaking with me. I assure you I will do whatever I can to find Karen."

CHAPTER 30

Deciding to locate Karen Martin before calling Cain, Ronnie Glick drove back to Broome.

Clean-shaven and dressed in tan cargos, t-shirt, and sneakers, he stood among the crowd gathered outside the sheriff's office. He pulled his khaki *'life is good'* cap down over his eyes and listened to the conversation around him.

Since his earlier visit, the town had filled with tourists drawn to the trails and shopping. But the real attraction was the mystery regarding the cause of death and the identity of the body found off the main hiking trail.

From the information swirling through the crowd, Glick learned the victim was a young woman, eighteen years old. When he heard someone say the Martins were brought to the medical examiner's office, Glick was surprised. He never expected the girl to turn up dead.

Ambling away from the crowd, he walked to a pub, and after scanning the menu in the window, went inside.

***

I left the Martins feeling like I gave more information than I received. At least they verified the body in the morgue was Mary Wells. Doctor Clancy was set to complete the autopsy. Based on ID from Daniel Martin, the medical examiner would contact several dentists in Stowe for records to verify her identity.

In spite of all the evidence of abduction, Sarah and Daniel Martin still held hope Karen was safe. Karen's backpack was found where the girls had planned to camp. Other than that, the campsites yielded no other clues as to what happened between the time they arrived at their destination, which was still not determined, and when Wells' body was discovered.

I'd been up and out since early morning. The coffee the Martins offered helped to keep me going, but I needed a meal. I drove back into the town square. I had my heart set on a hungry man dinner of steak and potatoes. Next to the small café where I lunched was a pub style restaurant, the Grog and Hog. According to the list of fare in their window, ribs and pulled pork were their specialty. But a blackboard menu standing out front advertised a twelve-ounce prime rib.

My mouth watering, I pushed through the wood and etched glass door. The inside was more hip than I expected for a rural, small-town establishment. The high beamed and tin ceiling gave it a spacious feel. A shelf around the perimeter held empty beer bottles of many domestic and imported labels. The walls alternated between tan brick and berry colored wallpaper.

Photographs of hikers on trails and in the mountains hung above every table. Upholstered chairs and teak tabletops with iron bases took up one side of the large room. The bar, booths, and high-top tables were on the other. Two front windows let in ample light so the atmosphere was upbeat and modern.

A young girl rushed by, telling me to sit wherever I liked. I passed the long, well-stocked bar and opted for a booth in the back. I slipped into the seat, stretched out my legs in front of me, and grabbed the beer list. Someone came to stand at the end of the table.

"So, what do you recommend?" I asked, still perusing the list.

"I recommend you leave Broome and let me do my job."

I recognized the husky voice. Raising my eyes to Madeline Grange, I caught her signature glare. She still wore her uniform, except the top two shirt buttons were undone and her hair hung loose at her shoulders. I could tell by her expression she wasn't in a social mood. I ignored it.

"Sheriff Grange, would you care to join me? Then you can tell me why I'm being run out of Dodge."

Her mouth twitched, and I saw what I thought might be the making of a smile. The sheriff removed her cellphone from her pants pocket, placed it on the table, and slid into the seat opposite me. Her lips tight, she resumed her glare. I gave her my most disarming grin, which had no effect whatsoever.

"By the way, thanks for the nod about the girl not being Karen Martin. I appreciate it."

"Really? Is that why you intruded on the Martins, interfering in my investigation in the process?"

"Interfere? How was my visit to the Martins' interfering?"

Her glare deepened. I was not intimidated. Her eyes relaxed and she sighed.

"As you undoubtedly know, Daniel Martin has identified the girl as their daughter's friend Mary Wells."

"Yes."

"Karen Martin is still missing. She is a person of interest in the investigation."

A person of interest meant suspect.

"Do you think Karen had something to do with her friend's death?"

"I can't rule anything out. In fact, the Martins are also of interest at this point. Can you understand why I didn't appreciate you speaking with them?"

I shrugged. "Those scenarios never occurred to me."

Even though I said that to Sheriff Grange, they did, but I didn't believe the Martins could murder their daughter and her friend. I wasn't so sure about Karen Martin. With parents like Grayson and Maxwell, there's no telling what psychosis she might have inherited.

"With all due respect, Sheriff, why didn't you instruct them not to speak about the case? And if they're suspects, why is there no police detail on them?"

"I did instruct them. I also thought you'd come to see me first. We have limited resources and haven't charged them with anything. I sent a deputy to check on them, and they told him you'd been there."

"How can I help?"

"I'd appreciate it if you would stay out of my way." Sheriff Grange's tone was light but strained. I knew she was under a lot of pressure.

"I still have a job to do," I said. "Even though I know where Karen Martin lives, I have to ascertain she's alive. I have a client to inform."

Crossing her arms on the table, Sheriff Grange leaned toward me.

"If the autopsy shows the girl we found died as a result of foul play, then I have a killer to catch."

As a former police officer, I understood the sheriff's position. Again, I offered her my expertise.

"Sheriff, as you admitted, you don't have enough resources for an investigation that encompasses such a wide area. I could be of service to you. You never know what I might turn up."

"Maybe," she said as her cell vibrated. I could tell someone was informing her on some aspect of the case. When she ended the call, she looked as if she was debating on whether or not to tell me what was going on. "That was Brimmer. A young man came forward to say his girlfriend and her friend went camping the other night and he hasn't heard from them. He became concerned when he heard about the body we discovered. I need to question him. He says he knows where they made camp."

"That's great. Funny, the Martins never said anything about a boyfriend."

"He says they didn't know. They just started seeing each other. Steve got the impression he was more serious than Karen was. He said she's very independent."

I grinned at the woman sitting across from me. I knew the type.

"Would you mind if I tagged along?"

"I'd prefer to question him myself. But I'll call you when I'm done, and we'll take it from there."

"Okay," I said. It was more than I expected.

I planned to do some poking around in the woods. The sheriff closed Moose Horn Trail. Still, that left a lot of outlying territory to cover—areas beyond the designated campgrounds.

I assured Sheriff Grange I wouldn't speak with any more of her persons of interest and would wait for her call.

The waiter came to take my order, which the sheriff took as her cue to leave. I sipped my beer and watched with pleasure as she strode toward the door. She acknowledged a few patrons along the way, twisting around to share a few words with a man at the bar. He touched her elbow, leaned in, and whispered something to her. I could feel my brows knit together and my lips tighten.

Madeline Grange laughed. She had a beautiful smile, which disappeared from her face the instant she caught me watching her. Had she seen my disapproval? Or was it something I hadn't felt in ages—jealousy? She turned and left.

CHAPTER 31

Dead men tell no tales. The saying echoed in Cain's head. *And dead women.*

He started to pour himself a drink and then thought better of it. *That's what got me in this mess to begin with—I need to keep a clear head.*

But he didn't want to think clearly. He didn't want to think about what, in a state of desperation and inebriation, he'd done. In spite of his arrangement with Crocker, Cain was shocked when he came across an internet news story about the death of a young woman in Broome.

He had told him not to kill the girl. *Didn't I?* Cain tried to remember his last conversation with Crocker. *"I'll do whatever is necessary." Shit.*

Douglas Cain always had an eye on the Martins, wherever they lived. He knew exactly where to send Crocker. The mercenary said he had found an abandoned property, *"perfect for what I have in mind."*

Cain didn't want to know how Crocker planned to deal with Holt. He didn't care. *Who am I kidding? Why send in a killer if you don't expect anyone killed?*

Cain reasoned that if Holt was out of the way, he could handle Maxwell. But the discovery of the young woman's body threw Cain's mind into turmoil. He needed to verify Karen Martin was still alive and had tried to contact Crocker again, without success. *"I'm done talking to you. Don't call me again."* There was little consolation in knowing whatever Crocker did would be quick, clean, and untraceable to him. *God, I hope so.*

And where the hell is Glick? Ronnie Glick's car showed up at his garage. So far, though, he had no word from the retired police officer.

His mind raced from one problem to another. *What's up with Todd?* He began to think Grayson had overreacted to Janet Maxwell's attendance at the fundraiser. It had done nothing to hinder the success of the event. Grayson had made another impromptu speech before thanking everyone and wishing all a safe trip home. The senator's earlier restiveness caused by Maxwell's appearance waned as the night wore on, which allowed Cain to relax. If that was even possible.

Grayson's change in demeanor had puzzled the lawyer. One minute he was chastising Cain for not handling Maxwell, the next he's toasting his success and telling Cain everything will work out.

What the hell happened? Well, I'm not a murderer. No matter what Grayson thinks he wants.

CHAPTER 32

Ronnie Glick slunk down in the booth at the Grog and Hog and waited for the waitress to bring him another beer.

He had panicked when Lucas Holt breezed past him and slipped into the next booth. Glick had almost felt the pain of retaliation the PI would undoubtedly inflict on his body if he had recognized him. The North Carolina PI was all bold-and-bluster when he had backup, but a one-on-one with the six foot three investigator should be avoided at all cost.

Since his last meeting with Holt, Glick had cut his hair, shaved his mustache, and donned lighter clothing. *He won't know me.* He hoped and prayed. He also turned in the Jeep for a sedan with local plates.

Glick's attention peaked when the sheriff joined Holt. They spoke in low tones, but he was able to catch a few words. *So the girl in the morgue is not Karen Martin.*

He was about to get up and search out the waitress for his check, when the sheriff rose to leave. An agonizing half hour passed before Holt finished his meal. Holt slid from his booth. Glick's heart raced when the PI stopped beside him, rummaging in his pocket for change. A couple of coins dropped to the floor. Holt bent to scoop them up. Glick could feel Holt's eyes on him. He had nowhere to go trapped in the booth.

"Hey," Holt said.

Ronnie Glick broke into a sweat as a hot rush of terror washed over him. He swallowed hard and waited for Holt to make a move. The PI spoke.

"Nice hat."

Glick raised a shaky hand. "Thanks," he mumbled without looking up. He watched Holt leave the pub.

Whew. Life is good.

***

This bad situation can only get worse.

In his Manhattan office, Douglas Cain yanked the tie from his neck and struggled to maintain his composure.

He couldn't breathe. The mounting stress of what Crocker would do or had already done drained his energy and consumed his thoughts. The lawyer wiped sweat from his brow with the back of his hand. He pulled out his cellphone and, for the fourth time that day, entered Ronnie Glick's number. To Cain's surprise, his rogue employee answered.

"Glick, why haven't you returned my calls," he shouted into the phone. "Where the hell are you?"

"Sorry about that, sir. I've been working the

case."

"What case?" Cain couldn't believe the balls on Glick. "You don't have a case! Where are you?"

"In Pennsylvania, Broome to be exact."

"How..." A flash of memory reminded the lawyer of his last conversation with Glick. *Shit.* "Why are you there?"

"Doin' my job, sir."

"Your job was to get your ass back to New York City. You're fired, Glick. Come get your car and go home to North Carolina."

A moment of silence hung between them. Cain could hear the former officer suck in a deep breath and blow it out again, causing an annoying whiz in the lawyer's ear.

"You might want to reconsider, Mr. Cain." Glick said in a calm southern twang. "I think you should know what's going on here."

Finally getting through to Glick should have been a relief. Instead, he grew more anxious; his nerves were too raw to relax. He didn't trust the North Carolina ex-officer to follow through with anything he asked of him. But he was desperate and had no other options.

Cain stood, rounded his desk, and paced across the gold and red Aubusson carpet to a window. He peered down at the dizzying myriad of people walking up and down Fifth Avenue. He closed his eyes and asked, "What's going on?"

Glick gave Cain an abbreviated account of the events of the past couple of days, including a version of his encounter with Holt. Douglas Cain listened, while at the same time deciding on what to do next. Karen Martin may still be alive. The fact another young woman died was a complication he hadn't counted on. Crocker had been sloppy, which was totally out of character. Cain needed to stop him before the whole situation was brought to light and traced back to him—and Grayson.

"Does the local law enforcement have any idea what happened to the dead girl or Karen Martin?" asked Cain.

"Not as far as I can tell. They're scouring the area for evidence and the missing girl, but so far, nothing."

"What about Holt?"

"He's here now. Not sure how he found out the Martins were in Broome. He's as lost as the sheriff. She's thwarting his efforts and pretty much told him to get out of town."

That was a break for Cain. Having finally reached Glick and having a good idea where Crocker was, his next step was to make contact. It was only a matter of time before the sheriff and Holt figured things out. He also knew enough about Lucas Holt to know the PI would not go away.

"Glick, you might be able to redeem yourself by doing exactly what I tell you."

CHAPTER 33

There were two places to stay in Broome. One, a small hotel in the square, and the other a bed and breakfast conveniently located at the edge of the woods, not far from Doc Clancy's haunted house. I had booked a room at the latter.

I kept my promise to Sheriff Grange and passed on visiting the medical examiner. The proprietors of Sweet Slumber B&B, an older couple, lived in a separate extension of the house. I had an earlier conversation with the innkeeper, Mr. O'Donahue, about Broome, its history and terrain. He mentioned there were many unused trails in the mountains around Broome. One in particular was behind his property. If you hiked deep enough, you could pick up another unused trail, which connected with Moose Horn. These trails would be worth exploring. The O'Donahues were busy with another guest. They waved as I passed on my way to my first-floor room, which was at the back of the second biggest house in Broome.

The home, a sturdy colonial, had wood floors

covered with area rugs that didn't squeak under my weight. My room was comfortable, with a view of the woods. I checked the relatively new door and windows. They opened and closed easily and quietly. I'd be able to come and go without alerting the others in the house.

I'd settled in the room, my stomach sated, when Mrs. O'Donahue came to tell me the sheriff was there to see me. I stopped at the doorway to the sitting room. Her back to me, Maddie Grange stood at one of the bookcases, scanning the inn's offerings. She'd changed from her uniform into dark jeans and a white, filmy blouse contoured at the waist, which hung loose to the top of her hips. Under the yellowish light in the ceiling, her red hair glowed like a tequila sunrise. She turned.

"Oh, how long were you standing there?"

Relaxed in my observation of the sheriff, I'd leaned on the doorframe and had folded my arms across my chest. I pushed off the jamb and moved toward her.

"Not long." I motioned to the sofa. "Would you like to sit?"

She shook her head. "No thanks, this won't take long. Mr. Holt…"

I interrupted. "Call me Lucas, and may I call you…"

She looked like she was about to refuse my offer of familiarity, but instead smiled.

"Okay, Lucas, and you can call me Sheriff."

She laughed before I could gauge whether or not she was kidding. "You look like a boy who was told he couldn't have dessert. Sure, call me Maddie."

At that moment I wished Karen Martin was home safe and sound and I could spend time with this woman in a more personal and enjoyable way. *Timing is everything.*

"What brings you here, Maddie?"

Deciding to sit, she dropped into one of the oversized club chairs in the room and crossed one long leg over the other.

"I said I would update you after I interviewed Karen's boyfriend."

"You said you'd call." I gave her a wry smile, and I could see the hint of a blush.

"Yes…in any case, the boyfriend, Sam Winters, showed us an old campsite off the main trail."

"And?" I asked, eager for some good news.

Maddie shook her head as she spoke. "Nothing. Someone did a thorough job of cleaning up. The only tracks were coming and going directly from the trail. We determined those belonged to the girls and Sam."

"That means we're not dealing with an amateur."

"I agree. We searched a radius of fifty yards out from the edge of the camp. We found evidence in a few places where someone could have traveled to the campsite. It doesn't narrow it down enough, though. I have men searching anyway. We could spend days scouring the area."

"Thanks for keeping me posted."

"I wish there was more to tell."

Maddie rose from the chair and walked to the inn's front door. I opened it and followed her outside to her car. After she slipped inside, I shut the door. The window was open. I leaned in.

"What will you do now?" she asked.

"I'm going to hike some of the unused trails Mr. O'Donahue mentioned. I don't want to step on your toes."

"Sounds good," Maddie said, and started the engine. "Between the both of us, we should cover a lot of ground. Don't forget to return the favor and let me know what you find."

"You bet," I said, and watched the sheriff drive off in a cloud of dust along the gravel driveway.

Planning to get a few hours' rest before beginning my own search of the woods, I set my phone alarm for 5:00 a.m.

Sleep didn't come easy. Partly due to thoughts of Maddie Grange and why she'd come to deliver the results of the interview with Sam in person. I hoped she was motivated by the same feelings that caused me to be glad she did.

Once thinking returned to my brain, my restlessness came from the realization that as more time passed, the more likely I would find a corpse.

***

Oh God, it reeks. Like something died. Karen tried to stretch her bound legs. Every joint and muscle ached when she moved—and when she didn't. Drawing a deep breath, she regretted it when the foul odor of rotted leaves, animal droppings, and her disheveled, unwashed captor assaulted her nose. The rancid stench nauseated her.

Opening her eyes and choking back a sob, she fought to remember how she came to be there.

Who is this monster?

The man who sat against the opposite wall of the tomblike space slept with his head dropped at one shoulder. A small puck light rested on the dirt floor near his leg, illuminating his huge frame. Some of his long, black hair escaped its binding and hung over one eye and cheek. Karen shuddered at the sight of his reddened, cratered face, made more frightening by errant, scraggly whiskers and a large bent nose. She closed her eyes, not able to look at him any longer.

Karen took quiet, shallow breaths so as not to wake him and to calm her nerves. It was no use. *What does he plan to do with me?* Her tongue felt dry and gritty. *I'm hungry and so thirsty.* Tears drizzled over Karen's cheeks to her mouth and chin. She licked the salty drops and swallowed. Her throat burned with bile. *I won't let him see that I'm frightened.* She wiggled her bound hands to free them as her mind flooded with more questions. One question rose above the rest. One she wanted to push to the back of her mind for fear of the answer. *What happened to Mary?*

***

Crocker woke from a nap to the angry eyes of Karen Martin.

Tonight, her mumbled efforts to goad him contributed to his exhaustion. His captive lay on her side facing him, still bound and gagged. She wore a man's long sleeve shirt, open at the front, over blue jeans. Both were filthy from the damp dirt floor. He sat up, leaning against rickety wooden shelves.

He whispered, "You can have an energy bar and a sip of water. No talking. Piss me off and you'll be bitchin' through a slit in your throat." He pulled the gag below her chin and fed her small bites.

When done, she rasped, "You stink."

Crocker yanked the gag back over her mouth. His eyes bore into hers. After eighteen hours of occasional short naps, he wasn't in the mood for her bullshit. He relished the thought of her begging when she realized she was being buried alive.

CHAPTER 34

Maddie Grange brushed her hair, pulled it back, and fastened it with a scrunchie. She washed her face and slathered it with moisturizer. The dark circles under her eyes made her groan. *I look like a hag. He probably noticed every line on my face. I definitely need more sleep.*

Comfortable in a cotton nightshirt, she flopped down on the bed, grabbed the remote, and turned on the TV. *I need to unwind first.* She flipped channels. At that late hour, the choices were limited to B movies, forty-year-old sitcoms, and the news. She switched off the television and opened the book she kept on her nightstand. She'd bought it a month ago and had only read twenty pages. Usually she was too tired to get through more than a page or two at night. *This should put me to sleep.*

After staring at the same sentence for five minutes, Maddie gave up and set the book aside. The death of the girl found in the woods consumed her thoughts. She hadn't been involved in investigating a suspicious death since her days in

Baltimore.

Too many violent and senseless killings were one of the reasons she made the decision to leave "Charm City" and settle in Broome. The other filled her with anger and terror every time she thought of it, so she rarely did.

Alex Clancy told her the mayor suggested he rule the death accidental since it's as likely as foul play. Of course, Mayor Strickland wanted the trail and campsites opened as soon as possible. Maddie would be very happy if it were an accident. But the fact another girl was missing was not a good sign.

She thought of Karen Martin—and Lucas Holt. Maddie was sure he wasn't telling her everything. There was more to this than a birth mother trying to find her biological daughter. She did some checking on Holt after he left her office. Sheriff Grange still had some contacts in Baltimore who in turn had contacts in New York. *This is not his usual type of case.*

Regardless, he had a high recovery rate for his clients and if she was honest, she could use his help. She had no doubt he wouldn't leave Broome until he'd done what he came for. At first, he'd rubbed her the wrong way. *He swaggered into my office looking all big-city. I could feel him sizing me up, wondering if I could handle the case.* He didn't know she had worked plenty of homicides in Baltimore. She was more than capable. Maddie sighed. *Be honest.* She was miffed when she heard he'd been to see the Martins. *I would have done the same thing.*

A picture of him at the Grog and Hog slouched

in the booth and studying the beer list flashed in her mind. She remembered the boyish grin he used to try to charm her and smiled at the memory.

Had she made a fool of herself going to see him instead of calling? He actually called her out on it. *Ugh.* No matter. She'd keep him close by. She needed his expertise—and he wasn't bad to look at either. Maddie shook her head to clear it. *Damn, I've lived in the woods too long.*

She picked up her book again, read half a page, and dozed. The book slipped from her hands onto the hard floor. She woke, turned the light off, and rolled onto her side to sleep.

CHAPTER 35

The day promised to be hot. The earlier I searched the woods, the better.

Dressed and ready to go in lightweight pants, a long-sleeved cotton shirt, and waterproof hiking boots, the only thing missing was some breakfast.

Mrs. O'Donahue rose early to prepare an urn of coffee and bake some muffins. I drank and ate quickly and managed not to encounter my hosts or any guests. I grabbed a backpack with some hiking essentials, slipped out a back door and veered to the right of the property to walk along a row of tall cedars.

The sun hadn't fully risen. I looked to the line of trees in the distance that marked the edge of the woods. Mr. O'Donahue said there were still remnants of a sign that indicated the entrance to Red Fox Trail. An old Broome trail map in hand, I flipped to the section already marked to show the approximate distance from the B&B to the trailhead.

I'd gone fifty yards when I spotted a small

clearing just beyond the cedars. Years of weeds sprouted through what was once a blacktopped parking area. Farther beyond the trees lay a crossroad the map told me was Chambers.

I still wanted to talk to Doctor Clancy. If Mary Wells was murdered, the details of her death could shed some light on the perpetrator. And if Mary and Karen were together when Mary met her demise, there were three possible reasons for Karen's disappearance. Karen killed Mary and fled. Karen was injured or dead. Karen was alive and being held against her will. My gut told me Karen wasn't a killer. I was less certain she was alive. It would solve all of Grayson's problems if she were dead—and the body never found.

I thought about possible suspects. Glick was on my tail—undoubtedly hired by someone connected with Grayson. I'd given the ex-officer credit for throwing a few wrenches in my investigation, including the stunt in Smoulder. For all his bravado and threatening notes, I thought Glick capable of kidnapping, maybe—not murder. Perhaps Mary's death was an accident after all.

My mind was going in too many directions and time was of the essence. Karen was already missing longer than would be considered a reasonable timeframe for the recovery of a victim of a violent crime. For me, though, no timeframe was too narrow. It had been fifteen years since my daughter's kidnapping, and I hadn't given up hope. My ever-present desire to find Marnie drove my success in the victim recovery cases I'd accepted over the years.

I found the trail sign half hidden under tall fescue and poison ivy. A heavy growth of creeping vines and shrubs created a barricade at the entrance. In addition to the backpack, I'd strapped a sheathed short machete and holstered Glock to my waist. I cut through six feet of overgrowth before I could see a two-foot wide path that wound through the trees.

The sun rose and morning light broke through the treetops. I had to remind myself of the dire purpose for the hike as I began to enjoy the cool, crisp air and the fresh smell of the woods. A natural mulch of dead pine needles kept the small width of trail clear of grasses. I hiked for a half hour in a northwesterly direction, listening for nature's sounds of the wild. Sounds I learned to recognize from years of hiking and from my days as an Army Ranger and member of Delta Force.

I continued to follow the trail west and saw no evidence of recent activity. It was the day after the discovery of the body off Moose Horn Trail. I wondered why the Sheriff hadn't ordered a search of this area. In any case, I forged on until I noticed a fork in the road. Someone with an untrained eye would pass right by without noticing the awkward bend of the branches on some low shrubs. A few with fresh breaks at the ends lay a couple of feet away. Just beyond the shrubs was a path, tamped with dirt, pine needles, and leaves. I pulled out my machete and used it to brush some aside. It moved away easily, revealing a solid dirt path with a faint but discernible footprint.

Someone had taken the time to cover his tracks.

I consulted the map again and decided to continue westward, leaving the northbound fork for later. From that point on, no one had bothered to cover any tracks on the worn, trodden trail. The high canopy and low density of the trees allowed light and rain to disguise when someone used it last.

A short distance along, the trail widened into an open area that spread to the edge of a cliff. Below were the large backyards of a few houses abutting the mountain. I recognized the Martins' white saltbox and the red cars in the driveway. The clearing was an ideal spot for observation.

Although the area at the edge of the overlook had no signs of encampment, a twenty-foot walk north into the trees told another story. The ground was clean. Too clean. Someone had raked out any tracks—human or animal. The leaves, spread evenly or clumped in neat piles, looked unnatural.

I followed the path northward for ten feet and could see to where the tree line widened enough to allow the passage of a vehicle. Another look at the map revealed a trail crossing Farm Road a mile to the north. Easy access if someone was looking for a way to keep an eye on the Martins, but not necessarily convenient for abduction. Besides, the girl's body was found in a southwest location, nearer the campgrounds.

I hiked another few yards and scanned the area, poking and pushing loose vegetation with my machete. I widened my scope a few feet and saw something wedged in a shrub. It was a remnant of the wrapper of an energy bar. I put on latex gloves and bagged the possible evidence.

Returning to the trail, I searched until spotting a damp clump of dirt and leaves. I stabbed a leaf with my knife and brought it to my nose. It smelled of motor oil. I knew if I hiked far enough I would find tire tracks. The distance was too great to cover up all the evidence, especially if you were in a hurry. Convinced I'd discovered a surveillance site, the odds were high that, at some point, someone had confronted Karen Martin and Mary Wells.

I was torn as to which direction I should take to resume my search. I could continue west and connect with Moose Horn Trail, or head north and follow the trail to Farm Road. Chances were Sheriff Grange had already combed the area surrounding the crime scene and I would find little else. What I needed to do was find Karen Martin and the trail north was my best bet.

Holstering my machete and adjusting my backpack, I prepared for a mile-long trek. I'd only gone a few feet when I heard the rush of foliage and a distant thudding on the ground. The thought of a bear in the woods flashed through my mind. I pulled out my Glock and hid behind a tree.

The sounds grew louder and faster. As it drew closer, whatever it was began to pant and heave big gasps of breath. The second I realized it wasn't an animal, a man shot out from the trees onto the trail and passed me. He ran like the wind and turned his head every few seconds to look behind him. I knew if he kept running at his current speed, he'd probably plummet right off the edge of the clearing.

I sprang from my hiding place and caught up with him before he reached the overlook. He was much smaller than I was, and I easily tackled him to the ground.

He fought wildly and screamed, "Let me go. Someone's coming and he's gonna kill me!"

I turned the man onto his back and was shocked to see whom it was. "Glick!"

He recognized me too. His eyes widened with so much horror, I thought he'd faint. Did I instill that much fear in people? I found out in short order Glick was far more afraid of someone else.

"Holt, you gotta let me go. The guy is crazy. I need to tell the sheriff. Let me go. He'll kill both of us for chrissake!"

Still holding Glick down on the ground, I put my finger to my lip indicating quiet and listened. There was no sound other than an occasional bird chirping or the rustling of the tops of the trees. I looked down at Glick and noticed his changed appearance. I wondered how long he might have been on my tail without my knowing. His panic and claims of someone following him became suspect. I yanked his shirt collar with both hands, lifting his head toward me.

"Who's gonna kill you, Glick? I mean besides me, you little shit."

"I...I don't know who he is. But I know he's dangerous. When he saw me, he took a shot at me. I ran like hell."

"No one's following you. He wanted to scare you." I couldn't help smiling at the memory of terror on Glick's face.

"It's not funny, Holt. Look, you gotta let me go. I'm on a case. I have orders to report what I find to the sheriff. It's a matter of life and death."

"How about you tell me what you found or it'll be a matter of *your* life or death."

Glick opened his mouth to speak and stopped. His face looked as if he'd turned to stone. I'd heard the faint snap of twigs too.

I whispered, "Get up." I grabbed his arm and showed him the end of my muzzle. "And keep quiet."

Glick barely nodded and lifted himself off the ground. I led him to a tree away from the path and listened for more signs someone was there in the woods with us. Sweat poured down the ex-officer's face. He jumped back against the tree with the rush of some nearby bushes. I raised my gun and took aim just as a rabbit bolted in front of us.

"Goddammit," Glick muttered and wiped his face with his shirtsleeve.

"C'mon," I told him. "You and I are going to see the sheriff together."

Glick shook his head.

"Don't give me any trouble," I said through gritted teeth. "I'm using all my powers of self-control not to beat you to a pulp and leave you here to rot."

I turned Glick around and put my gun to his back. He stiffened, moved forward, and then stopped. He swung his head toward me.

"Holt, I think you or I should call the sheriff. By the time we get to town, the guy might be gone."

I hated to admit it, but Glick was right. I pulled out my cellphone. No service.

"It's a good idea, but we need to get to the

clearing up ahead before we can use our phones. In the meantime, tell me what you saw. Does it have anything to do with Karen Martin?"

"Yeah. But my orders are to go right to the sheriff."

I didn't know whether to trust this guy or not. If he had information that could lead me to Karen Martin, I needed to know right away.

"Listen to me. The girl's life may be in danger. Tell me what you saw. If you know where she is, tell me. I can't wait for the sheriff. I need to get to the girl as soon as possible."

We were fifteen feet from the edge of the overlook. Before we stepped from the woods, Glick stopped walking again.

"When we get the sheriff on the phone, I'll tell her what I know, then you'll know. You can do whatever you want with the information after that."

Glick wasn't so dumb after all. He'd found a way to protect himself from my anger.

"Who are you working for, Glick? Is it Douglas Cain?"

His expression was all the answer I needed. Still, he tried to deny it.

"I don't know who that is, and I'm not at liberty to say who hires me. Same as you, Holt."

Glick made a mistake and gave me a smug grin. I right hooked him in the chin and sent him flying against a nearby oak. I grabbed his shirt and pulled him to his feet.

"I'm all out of patience, Glick. Forget the sheriff. Tell me where the girl is now or you'll be leaving these woods on a stretcher." He looked like he didn't quite believe me so I hit him again. I prepared for another swing. That did the trick.

"Stop—stop! You're crazy too, Holt. Shit. Okay, there's a place a mile north of here."

"What place? C'mon, you asshole, I need details. Did you see the girl?"

"No, but I heard someone. Sounded like a girl. Then this huge, ugly son-of-a-bitch came outside, spotted me, and started shooting."

"Tell me exactly where this place is. Point to it on the map." I pulled out the map, opened it to where we stood, and showed it to Glick. He scratched his chin, taking a moment to scan it.

"Uh, there," he said and removed his fingers from his face and pointed to the spot on the map.

"Down!" I screamed, recognizing the suppressed shot from a high caliber rifle as it reverberated through the trees. I dropped to the ground and rolled for cover toward an oak.

The shooter took another shot, the bullet racing over my head as I burrowed deeper into the ground. His shots were too close to the mark given all the trees that blocked his aim. He was nearby. I pulled up, my back to the tree. Making sure Glick was not in the way, I sent a few rounds into the woods in the direction of the gunfire. I grabbed a pair of binoculars, but couldn't see any sign of the assailant.

Within minutes, police sirens blared in the distance. A resident living below the clearing must have heard the shots. I replaced the magazine in my gun and inched toward Glick, who took cover six feet from me.

"Glick, I hear the sheriff's cars. Glick." When he didn't respond, I rolled him over.

Ronald Glick lay still, his eyes wide and lifeless, a bullet in his head.

CHAPTER 36

Crocker raced toward the barn, hunched over and dripping sweat. He stopped and knelt in the brush to listen for movement behind him. Nothing.

Who was that skinny bastard?

Seeing an intruder at the tree line around the barn was a surprise. Seeing him talking to Holt was a shock to the system. *Did the skinny guy hear the girl scream? How much did he tell Holt?* In that moment, Crocker wanted to end the mission. He wanted kill the intruder, kill Holt, return to the barn, and finish the girl.

Then Crocker heard the police sirens.

I don't have much time before they search for me.

Not sensing anyone in pursuit, Crocker rose from a crouch and continued running. The trail was laden with low hanging branches that stung his face. Thick roots protruded from the soft dirt like dark tentacles reaching for his ankles. Crocker's mind raced through scenarios, rejecting each one as not practical, too risky, or not working with the end game he planned. He decided, given the current situation, his original plan still worked best.

Stopping at the edge of the trees, he again listened for hunters while inspecting the red barn. The silence was comforting. Earlier, Crocker had found a rake and used it to erase his tire tracks and nearly all of his footprints. The ground showed no evidence anyone had stumbled upon his refuge. The dilapidated barn and surrounding grounds looked as he left it.

Ten minutes. He would give himself ten minutes to calm the girl and setup the barn.

Rushing to the root cellar, Crocker brushed aside the camouflage and lifted the creaky wooden door. The steps down softened under his weight as he descended. The girl lay exactly as he left her. "Okay, listen. I'm going to give you another injection. You'll take a three-hour nap. I'll be back later. Sound good?"

Karen cringed, shook off his grip, and rasped over the gag, "Bastard."

"Ah. I like feisty women, but not today. *So shut the fuck up.*"

Crocker reached into his backpack and retrieved the syringe and vial. He inserted the needle and drew the clear fluid into the syringe, tapped out the air bubble and injected her with the contents. Crocker pocketed the empty syringe and exited the root cellar.

He again camouflaged the cellar door with thick branches and leaves. There was little time before the police would arrive. He hurried to the ladder at the center of the barn and climbed to the hayloft.

Opening the sliding door, he surveyed the surrounding area for an ambush. A humid gust of warm wind rushed past him. The line of oaks and low junipers barely budged. Crocker smelled the air for the exhaust of vehicles hiding nearby. No trace of fumes. He turned away and descended the ladder.

An idea flashed in Crocker's mind and he grinned. He walked over to the rough-hewn stanchion next to the ladder, took out his knife, and quickly carved a symbol.

Crocker jumped in the truck and backed it out of the barn. He stopped outside, opened the toolkit, and chose a claw hammer and some nails. He nailed the sliding front doors shut.

His final task made him smile. He walked to the woods behind the barn and retrieved the two empty cans of gasoline.

Time's up. He ran to his truck and drove away.

CHAPTER 37

My first reaction when I realized Glick was dead was to leave him for the sheriff and head north. If Glick's killer had kidnapped Karen Martin and she was still alive, he would need to get back to her. The fact he followed Glick meant the girl was some place secure. I needed to find that place. I feared the worst—that I wouldn't make it in time.

I should have expected Broome law enforcement's quick arrival, but was still surprised to see Chief Deputy Brimmer barrel through the trees in his police car. Brimmer didn't bother to ask what happened. He called Doctor Clancy, who arrived promptly to attend to the body. A few minutes later Sheriff Grange arrived at the scene. I groaned as I thought of all the evidence destroyed in the process of the emergency response.

The sheriff exited her car, eyeing me as she made her way toward Clancy. She squatted down next to the medical examiner. Clancy spoke in soft tones while pointing to parts of Glick's body. I moved closer. Maddie Grange rose. "Let me see your gun and your hands, please."

I pulled my gun from its holster and handed it to her, then held out both hands, palms up.

Maddie examined my gun and then my hands. "Turn them over, please." Her eyes widened at the bruises on my right knuckles. I knew what she was thinking.

"I admit I hit him, but I didn't kill him. You just have to find a shell casing to determine the shot wasn't fired from my gun."

Maddie gave the scene a cursory glance. "Brimmer, check for shell casings." She turned back to me. "Where did the shots come from?"

I pointed to the general area. Brimmer nodded and headed in that direction with a couple of volunteer deputies. I didn't know whom we were dealing with, but I knew he was a pro. The bullet hit Glick right between the eyes. He must have gone down with the first shot. From what I'd discovered while hiking in the woods and the precision of the bullet in Glick's head, I believed the killer had some military training. If that was the case, Broome's country cops were no match for him. They'd need all the help they could get. I showed the sheriff the approximate place on the map Glick pointed out before he was shot. Maddie stopped the deputy and gave him additional orders to search for the sniper, then turned to me. "Let's go." She asked for my machete and then ushered me into her car and drove to town.

I used the time to collect my thoughts and get my story straight—which was somewhat straightforward. I was hiking in the woods, met

Glick, who said he was being followed, and bang, someone shot him. I gave her my thoughts on the skill level of the perpetrator.

***

In her office, Sheriff Grange drummed her fingers on her desk. She watched me through slits formed with both eyelids. I had given her my straightforward story and waited for her response.

She gave up the drumroll and leaned back in her chair.

"I have a feeling I wouldn't be wrong to assume there's a strong connection between you and the deaths of two people in my town."

"I wasn't even in Broome when the girl died, and I didn't know Ronald Glick."

"You may not have known him personally, but there's a connection. We found a black sedan, rented to Glick."

"So?"

"So, inside was a notebook with some very interesting details. Did you know he was tailing you?"

Leave it to Glick to screw me even after he's dead. If I said I didn't know, I would look like an amateur. If I said I did, I'd have to admit to a connection. I decided to go with something from column A and column B.

"I knew someone was following me. I didn't know why."

"And you had no interest in finding out why? C'mon, Lucas, do I look like an idiot?"

In fact, Madeline Grange looked rather attractive. She still wore her uniform buttoned to the neck, but her unbound hair brushed her shoulders and neck like fiery feathers. My thoughts must have shown on my face. She pushed her hair behind her ears and turned away from me to glance out the window, which afforded me another nice view. I gathered my wits and thought Scully's remark about the last time I was with a woman was stuck somewhere in my subconscious.

"Sheriff, it doesn't matter if there's a connection. What matters is we both want Karen Martin found."

"Yes, and you still haven't told me the real reason you need to find her. It's more than a coincidence that a New York City PI comes to a remote Pennsylvania town in search of someone's daughter, who then disappears, and two people are murdered."

"Karen Martin was missing before I came to Broome."

"I suspect you're not the only one looking for her. And that leads me to wonder who Karen Martin is? Who are her biological parents?"

"You know I can't say without betraying confidentiality, Madd—"

"Stop!"

I could almost see the steam rise out of Maddie's nose and ears. This woman was clearly frustrated with me, so I let her continue.

"I've got two murders already, and it's a good bet there will be a third if you don't tell me what you know." She paused. "Look, I thought we were going to be honest with each other—share our information."

"Yes and regarding Glick's death, I told you all I know."

"*All* you know?"

"Yes. I have no idea who shot him. I'm not certain Glick's death is related to Karen Martin's disappearance. But my gut tells me it is."

"Yes, I believe so too."

"So, are we still friends?" I gave her a coy smile. "Can we work together?"

After a long pause, she said, "Yes." The word emerged as if it clung to her lips and was shoved out through her teeth with her tongue. I hid a self-satisfied grin.

"And I'm very happy to assist you, ma'am." I meant to be respectful, but sounded like I agreed to walk an old woman across the street. Maddie winced.

"So, now that we're *partners*," she said, appearing to mock the idea, "tell me what you know."

"What I know is we're on the clock. If Ronald Glick stumbled on the sniper's hidey-hole, the discovery may have triggered some panic in him. I'm not sure what he'll do next. I also know that working together on this will bring us closer to finding her."

The sheriff crossed her arms over her chest and then covered her mouth with one hand. I would have sworn I saw a flash of some horrific memory cross her mind. She shook her head as if to free herself of the thought and asked, "Do you think the girl is still alive?"

"I think we need to search the area to the north of where Glick was murdered before any more time passes. He saw something, and we need to know what."

"I've already sent Brimmer and a few deputies to scour the area north of Farm Road." She turned back to me. "There are a few abandoned buildings up there."

The sheriff's phone rang. From the one side of the conversation I heard, I knew it was Brimmer giving a report. I watched her face as she listened, and by her pursed lips and furrowed brow, I knew she didn't like what she was hearing. Disconnecting the call, Maddie pushed my gun across her desk and grabbed a set of keys.

"Lucas, we've got to go."

CHAPTER 38

As we drove away in the sheriff's Explorer, she filled me in on Brimmer's report.

"They're at an abandoned barn in the area Ronald Glick indicated on your map. There's evidence of someone having been there recently. But whoever was there is gone."

I shook my head in self-recrimination. I should have left Glick and gone after the sniper. Needing a diversion, I asked Maddie, "How long have you been Broome's sheriff?"

"Five years."

"And before that?"

"Baltimore. I was a homicide detective."

"Really? We have something in common."

Maddie glanced at me and smiled. "I know. How long have you been a PI?"

"Let's see…not quite fifteen years."

"Why'd you leave the police force?"

She'd checked me out. The conversation I started was becoming a Q & A and I'd rather be the one asking the questions.

"It's a long story, and we don't have enough time now."

She shrugged, accepting my non-answer. We drove the rest of the way in silence.

The sheriff knew exactly where she was going and we arrived in minutes. We turned off Farm Road onto a narrow lane edged by a row of overgrown shrubs. The tall weeds and grass pressed into the gravel on the lane showed more than one vehicle had passed through.

The remnants of an old ranch-style house stood a few yards from the road. A barn lay ahead at the end of the lane. Sheriff Grange pulled up next to Brimmer's police car, got out, and scanned the area for her deputy. I left the car and stood beside her.

"Where is everyone?" I asked. The fact no one was there to meet us made me uneasy.

"I don't know. I told Brimmer not to go anywhere until I got here."

"How many did you send with him?"

"Two others. Mullen and Delaney. Mullen grew up here and knows the mountains and trails better than anyone. Delaney has worked with me since I came to Broome and is one of my best volunteers."

"I'm going to take a look around," I said.

"Okay, then we'll go inside together," Grange said and told me not to wander.

She tapped her holstered gun, as if to make sure it was there, before she walked away. I moved to the front of the building and stepped back to take a good look. The barn was massive and a tired, worn red that blended with the tall oaks surrounding it.

The main door was jammed shut. I didn't bother

trying to open it. Circling the building, I noticed two Dutch doors, one on each side. Upon closer inspection, I found someone had removed the nails that held one closed. Whoever did it had come prepared; the job was clean and efficient. Sheriff Grange met me at the door as I finished my examination.

"That the way in?" she asked.

"Looks like it. Ready to go inside?"

She nodded. I opened and held the door for her. The sheriff pulled her weapon before entering. I did the same and followed.

Except for the stalls that lined one wall and the loft, the inside was one huge room. The ceiling, held in place by trusses connected to thick square posts, was spotted with holes. Strewn with old dried straw, the floor crackled under our feet.

Anyone inside would hear us. Chances were the sniper and his hostage were gone, but Brimmer and company still hadn't shown up, so we used caution.

"I'll cover you," I whispered to Sheriff Grange.

She holstered her gun for a moment to pull out a flashlight. Light in one hand and weapon in the other, she moved forward.

A canopy of trees prevented daylight from entering random openings left by rotted patches of shingles in the roof. After a cursory scan of the inside with her flashlight, Sheriff Grange headed for a fixture hanging from a rafter, and pulled the attached string.

A low-watt yellow bulb cast an eerie glow on the single spindled-backed chair underneath it. Several large drops of blood lay on the seat.

"Think it's fresh?" Sheriff Grange asked.

"Can't be sure, but if pressed, I'd have to say yes. And someone placed this chair intentionally under the only light source in the place. My guess is our guy tied the girl to it."

"So, you think it's her blood."

"It's impossible to know. Even though I was able to get off a few shots, I have no idea if they hit the guy. Did your men find any blood when they searched the woods where Glick was shot?"

"No. But the sniper didn't necessarily travel a straight path away from the scene."

The sheriff shone her light on the rough-hewn post behind the chair—on something etched into the wood—something familiar to me.

"You see this?" she asked, pointing to a triangle with a vertical dagger through it. "Isn't that the sign for—?"

"Delta Force," I answered before she could finish the question.

"Lucas, what's your feeling about him?"

"Off the top of my head, based on how Glick was killed and what I've seen here and on the trails, this guy is a pro."

"A hitman?" The sheriff shook her head. "That doesn't make sense. A hitman rarely kidnaps his target. And besides, who would hire an assassin to kill a young woman who has no enemies?"

I left the question unanswered and moved to the stalls and made a quick check of each one. They were empty. Only thing left to search was the loft. I climbed the ladder as the sheriff stood below shifting her torso back and forth, her gun still drawn. All the trap doors were closed, each topped with a clump of brittle hay. One pile caught my eye as it looked arranged—a neat mound compared to the flattened masses atop the other four doors.

I hesitated to stick my arm into it in case someone decided to hide a bear trap among the straw. Instead, I grabbed a pitchfork that leaned against the wall and prodded the hay. Three jabs and the pitchfork came up empty. I threw piles of hay to the side. Before I could stop the motion of another jab, I heard a slight buzz. At the same time, I felt the tines penetrate an object. I pulled upward and tossed the pitchfork, and what was attached, into another pile of straw.

"Maddie, run!" I yelled.

I slid down the rungs of the ladder and grabbed a stunned Sheriff Grange by the arm. The soft buzz was now a loud frenzy of insects I could see swirling around the hayloft.

"What's the matter?" she yelled as I dragged her behind me.

"Hornets. Run!"

"Hornets? What the hell—"

"C'mon—outside!"

We exited the barn, closed the door after us, and ran a few yards away. I turned and saw a stream of the large wasps flying out through the roof.

"There were hornets up there? Don't you know better than to stir up a hornet nest?"

"It was an accident. The damn thing was hidden in a pile of hay."

"Just your luck." Maddie Grange smiled.

"Nothing lucky about it," I said. "I'm sure

someone put it there for us to find. It's a message."

"A message? For who?"

"For me."

CHAPTER 39

Before the sheriff could ask why I thought the etching and hornets were meant for me, Brimmer and his deputies trudged out through the trees. Maddie Grange turned, placing her hands on her hips.

When they were within hearing distance, she shouted, "Where the hell have you been?"

Brimmer trotted closer. "Sorry, Sheriff. We noticed a worn path on the other side of the lane heading toward the house. By the depth of the footprints it was someone large or perhaps one person carrying another. We wanted to check it out."

"And what did you find?" she asked.

"Nothing. We followed the tracks through the woods and wound up right where you saw us come out. The trail led us nowhere."

Sheriff Grange scanned the property. "Did you search the house?"

Brimmer nodded. "Yeah, thought it might fall down around us. We were careful, though. Nothing inside. No sign anyone has been there."

I looked at the sheriff, who remained quiet. Focused on the ramshackle building, she gnawed on her lower lip. Something was on her mind. She hadn't informed Brimmer or the others about my theory of a message. The clock was ticking away so I prompted a response.

"What's our next move, Sheriff?"

Still staring at the neglected house, she started at the sound of my voice. She gave me a quick glance and then turned to Brimmer. "Steve, this guy can't have gone far. See if you can find the vehicle he used—a truck or SUV. He may have tried to hide it off road somewhere."

"My guess is its black," I offered. "And it will have local plates. He'll want to blend in."

Sheriff Grange nodded her agreement and continued to instruct Brimmer, "Drive up to the north route. Check any trailheads and vehicle access roads into the woods heading south."

"Sure thing, Sheriff." Brimmer motioned to Mullen and Delaney and then noticed the activity at the roof of the barn. "What's going on up there? Looks like a swarm of wasps."

"Yeah," the sheriff said to Brimmer. "There's a hornets' nest in the loft."

"Really? We didn't see one when we checked inside."

"It was hidden," I said. "Good thing for you, you didn't find it. They can do some nasty damage."

"Sounds like you've had personal experience," Brimmer said.

"Not me, but someone I knew."

"Wow, hope he's okay," Brimmer sounded sincere. "Getting stung by an army of hornets would make me crazy, if it didn't kill me first."

I didn't respond aloud, but I doubted the person I knew was okay. In fact, far from it on so many levels. Remembering the event that was so long ago I'd all but forgotten, I could hear Crocker's harsh threat.

"Holt, I know you did this. I'll never forget. You won't know when or how, but I promise somehow you'll pay."

He was out there somewhere. Watching. I could feel it. But it was daylight, and I wasn't alone. Was Karen still alive? If Crocker was Cain's hired gun, would the lawyer have given the order to kill Grayson's daughter?

I didn't doubt Cain had any reservations about killing me if it was to save the senator from scandal. But Crocker may have decided on his own plan. He had the chance to put a bullet in my head and chose not to. He wanted me to know the executioner and the reason for my death. I had to assume Karen was not dead, and to save her, I had to play the assassin's game.

I needed to come back after dark. Alone.

Brimmer left to scour the area for Crocker's vehicle. I thought even if they found it, there would be nothing of use in it. A professional assassin doesn't leave anything behind. Then again, since Crocker had turned the job into a personal vendetta against me, he may have slipped up.

Sheriff Grange walked toward the house and stopped ten feet away. I came up beside her. "What's on your mind, Maddie?"

She looked at me, and I could have sworn I saw tears in her eyes. She blinked them back. "What's on my mind? Finding that girl."

"You seem preoccupied with the house. Brimmer said no one had been inside."

"I know, but I think I should see for myself."

I followed Maddie up onto the wooden front porch, which hadn't been treated in two decades. Infested with termites, some planks looked like weathered lace. "Be careful where you walk. This porch could fall out from under you. It's a shame. Looks like it must have once been a nice property."

"It was. A long time ago."

I could hear the catch in her voice. Maddie pushed through the door into the house. There were a few pieces of furniture scattered throughout. Dingy gray curtains hung at the windows. Three small bedrooms off to one side were empty. She moved quickly from room to room, hesitating for a moment in a tiny pink one.

"Little girl's room," I stated the obvious.

"Color is awful," Maddie said. "I hate pink."

She brushed past me, headed for the kitchen, and was about to exit the back of the house when her cell phone buzzed. Maddie listened, nodding to me as she said into the phone, "Okay, have it brought to town. See you back there." She ended the call.

"They found a black truck. A rental. Probably belongs to our guy." She scanned the kitchen. "We're done here, Lucas."

226

CHAPTER 40

Perched high above with a clear view of the barn and house, Crocker had watched from a tree as Holt and the sheriff moved about the property.

He panicked after the deputies searched the house and left. The sheriff had taken an interest in the old building and surrounding area. He worried she would decide to search all the grounds. He wasn't ready for them to find the girl yet—if ever.

When they had emerged from the house, Crocker followed Holt through his binoculars as they walked to their car. The sheriff slid behind the steering wheel. Holt paused before getting inside. When the PI raised his head toward the treetops, a rush of excitement had washed over the assassin. Holt seemed to look directly at him.

***

Fixing the grappling hook to a heavy branch, Crocker dropped a rope and, after checking its grip on the wood, slipped down to within eight feet of the ground. He cut the rope just above his head and dropped onto a soft mound of brush and leaves piled at the tree's base.

Crocker ran to the root cellar to check on Karen Martin and prepare for his confrontation with Lucas Holt.

CHAPTER 41

Convinced Crocker held Karen Martin somewhere nearby, I didn't want to leave the property north of Farm Road. I was sure if we continued to search the grounds and found her, it would have been difficult to keep her safe from the sniper's bullet. He could see us. But we couldn't see him. To even the playing field, I had to go back under the cover of darkness at a time when Crocker would tire of waiting for me.

Maddie was quiet for most of the way back to town. Entering the dilapidated house, I had the distinct feeling she'd been there before and knew the property. Strangely, she wouldn't admit it. I gave her every opportunity to share, but instead she'd given me a brief history of Broome's logging industry.

Was I reading too much into her mood? I could easily check who owned the small defunct farm. Maybe the county owned the property. I turned to Maddie.

"Is there a site map or survey available for that

property to see if there are other buildings—places you could keep a hostage?"

She shook her head.

"You're clever, Lucas, but I doubt it. It's an old place, and a lot of files went up in flames a couple of years ago at County Records. And even if there is a survey, it would take forever to dig it up. They aren't too organized over there."

An excuse. I could smell one a mile away.

"Maddie, I think you're hiding something. Remember, a young woman's life is at stake here."

"I know what the stakes are. You want to know who owns the property? I do. And I'm angry as hell that there's every reason to believe it's being used to hold a young woman hostage."

"You own it? So you know the place well."

"Lucas, I haven't lived there since I was seven years old. If I knew where the girl was, I'd tell you."

We pulled up to the sheriff's office. Maddie jerked the Explorer into her reserved spot. She threw it into park and left the vehicle, slamming the door behind her. I followed her inside. She found Brimmer and began grilling him with questions about the black truck being stripped and examined in Marty's Garage and Body Shop.

Does everyone in Broome do double duty as a crime investigator?

Any further attempts to talk with the sheriff were thwarted when Daniel and Sarah Martin showed up demanding to know what was being done to find their daughter.

"Why haven't you found her?" Daniel Martin

shouted to the sheriff. "Who was killed on the hill behind our house? Does he have something to do with Karen's disappearance?"

"Mr. Martin, I want to assure you we are doing all we can to bring your daughter home."

"And just what is that?" Daniel Martin asked.

"We've narrowed down an area, but we have to be cautious."

"Oh my God! Why?" Sarah Martin gasped. "How dangerous is this person? Do you know who he is and why he has Karen?"

Maddie looked at me and so did the Martins.

"Mr. Holt." Sarah Martin stated my name as if their daughter's disappearance was my fault. Perhaps it was. I had a fleeting thought. *If only I hadn't taken this case.* I shook off the moment of guilt and tried to provide the Martins with a glimmer of hope.

"We're not sure where Karen is or why she was targeted. It's possible someone is trying to keep me from finding her. I don't believe someone's intent is to harm your daughter. But we have to take every precaution to make sure she is returned safely."

The Martins didn't appear appeased by my speech. In fact, they looked more terrified—and enraged.

"Are you saying, Mr. Holt, the real target here is you?" Daniel Martin's face was taut with anger. "Do you mean to say, our daughter's life is in danger because you came to Broome to find her?"

I didn't know what to say. Of course, that *was* the reason. At that point, I didn't dare mention who I thought had kidnapped Karen and in all likelihood had been responsible for Mary Wells' death. I gave Maddie a dark stare, thanking her for directing the Martins' wrath at me. She nodded, "you're welcome" and then took over the conversation, offering the Martins coffee along with assurance Karen would be found.

The Martins left and before I could speak to Maddie privately, Delaney drew her attention to some more information about Crocker's truck. I moved closer. She acknowledged me and allowed me to listen in. As I suspected, the vehicle was clean; there were no personal effects, no blood or trace evidence. So far, we had nothing to prove who killed Glick and Mary Wells.

"Sheriff, what about using dogs to find the missing girl?" Delaney asked.

"We don't have immediate access to trained dogs. Make some phone calls to see who has any available and how soon they can bring them here."

"The dogs are a good idea," I said. "But this guy is waiting for us. If we go in like gangbusters, he may open fire on us, the dogs, and ultimately kill the girl in the process. We need a more covert way of finding the killer and Karen."

Maddie nodded her agreement. "Let's arrange to get the dogs and use them if the situation warrants it."

"Okay, Sheriff, I'm on it," Delaney said and left the office.

"Where are Brimmer and Mullen?" I asked. "Back at the garage?"

"No, I gave them another assignment."

I waited for more explanation, but it didn't come.

"So should I assume I'm on my own again, Sheriff?"

"What are you talking about?" she asked and her eyes widened in surprise by my question.

"I thought we agreed to work as team," I said. "But you're not letting me in on all that's going on. I told you, I don't want to step on anyone's toes or cover ground that's already been covered."

"Lucas, this is my town and my search and rescue. I'll handle it the way I see fit. I don't need to 'let you in' on anything if I think it will impede the results I want."

I was dumbfounded.

"I thought we were working together. If that's not the case anymore..."

"It's not the case," she said. "I mean, I do need your help. As soon as I get reports from all my guys, we can discuss what to do next. In the meantime, it's late. We have to wait for daylight to continue searching the woods."

I wasn't sure if she was trying to placate me or if she meant to keep me in the loop. I had my own plan in mind and hoped to hell Maddie's "handling" wouldn't impede the results *I* wanted. The only thing I could do was trust that whatever she did wouldn't further jeopardize Karen Martin's life—or mine.

CHAPTER 42

She didn't know if she could trust him. Lucas Holt was smart and resourceful; his reputation preceded him, as she had found out. *He's not Sean.* Maddie wondered if she would ever be able to work with a partner again.

Staring out her living room window into the dark woods, thoughts of a killer out there holding a young woman captive sent shivers through her. *How could this happen? This is Broome. Nothing happens here.*

She had few resources and few people she could count on. Of course, she could rely on Steve Brimmer, and Peter Delaney, who at times seemed to be her shadow. But since she'd moved to Broome and become the sheriff, there hadn't been an opportunity to test their loyalty. Her life had never depended on them. Holt reminded her too much of Sean Kassel, her former undercover partner.

Maddie had been handpicked out of the academy to get cozy with Zach Jones, a lieutenant of Baltimore's infamous drug trafficker, Harry

Burnside. Sean already had spent time within the criminal organization. Maddie worked with him for two years before a bust gone bad exposed him as an undercover agent. He had tried to bargain for his life by giving up hers.

She owed her survival to Zach, who it turned out, she could trust more than her partner. He convinced Burnside that Sean lied to take the focus off himself. She thought about Zach and the livelihood he chose; it had made him a rich man.

Maddie let the shower's hot water wash away the memory and the tears that trickled down her face. In the end, she had left the organization, left Zach, and worked as a homicide detective until it was no longer safe to stay in Baltimore.

***

After eating a light dinner, Maddie stretched out on her sofa. She entered into a restless, dream-laden sleep, in which she was five, then fifteen, then twenty-five.

She dreamed of meeting Zach. It had been so easy for them to be together. She didn't have to pretend. It was real.

Maddie's slumbering body jerked as images raced through her mind. Someone pressed a gun to her head. Liar! Fraud! *She heard someone plead for her life.* Sean? *He was her partner. He was supposed to protect her. But it wasn't Sean; it was Zach.*

His back was to her as he spoke to Harry

235

Burnside. She could see the long muscular shape of his body; his broad shoulders—familiar but different. Now, Sean was speaking to Harry, offering to shoot her to show his loyalty. Son of a bitch. *Harry told him to go ahead.* Nooo! *Zach raised his gun and shot Sean, then turned and shot the man who gripped Maddie's arm and held the gun to her temple. Her knees buckled.* Zach! *He rushed to her before she fell to the floor. She looked up at him with grateful eyes. But it wasn't Zach. It was Lucas Holt.*

***

Shaken by the ominous dream, Maddie struggled with whether or not to call Lucas. She glanced at the clock. She had no doubt he would return to the farm to confront the madman who already murdered two people.

Before that morning, the last time she had been in the house north of Farm Road was when her father was dying. She had returned to Broome to say goodbye, though he didn't deserve the gesture.

Maddie could tell her father was glad she had come, but he couldn't bring himself to say he was sorry. Instead, he left her all his worldly belongings, a neglected, rundown property she had no interest in owning. So she let it continue to rot. It was a rotten place to live anyway—at least after her grandmother died.

When she had entered the house—her house—with Holt earlier that day, she imagined Grams was alive. She remembered the aroma of roasting chickens and baked pies. Her grandmother had delighted her with colorful stories of "the olden days" and lovingly offered advice. She smiled; she could always count on Grams for guidance.

Maddie moved about the sitting room of her cabin. Restless, she paced. Something niggled at the back of her mind—something about the house north of Farm Road. Grams had warned her to stay away. It wasn't safe. Maddie shook her head to clear it and sat in an old wooden rocker, the only piece of furniture she removed from the house. Grams chair. As she rocked, Maddie recalled with affection how together she and her grandmother had picked, hulled and preserved wild strawberries that grew in abundance.

A chill replaced the warmth of the moment and a sudden memory of homemade strawberry jam told Sheriff Grange where to find Karen Martin.

***

As he periodically had done over the last several hours, Crocker crept up the stairs of the cellar, raised the door an inch, and scrutinized the back of the house. Taking a deep breath, he edged the door up high enough to allow his head and waist above ground. He padded out into the deep shadow of the house, crouched, and ran to the wall.

If Holt is here, he'll be hiding in the perimeter, waiting.

Crocker wasn't too concerned about Holt killing him as long as the PI didn't know where the girl could be found. Entering the backdoor of the house, he moved to one of the bedrooms. He smelled the mold and mildew in the corners of the ceiling and felt the wood floor buckle beneath him. Peering out through a broken window, hoping to spot Holt, his head jerked left. He saw a bush quiver.

Well, I'll be damned.

"Lucas, you've lost more than a step or two," Crocker whispered to himself and cracked a smile, which turned to a wide grin. Then a memory flooded his thoughts; Lucas Holt had fooled him before.

An angry focus replaced the grin as he hurried to the kitchen. Crocker stepped back into the shadows behind the house, his boot crushing a chunk of glass from a broken window. He crept to the side of the house facing the shrubs. Crouching at the corner, he drew his Glock and peered around the edge. The trees' heavy canopy blocked the moonlight, but he could see the outline of someone sitting on their haunches watching the house. To Crocker's delight, the dark form was moving towards him. He drew a breath and stood still.

One more moment…Crocker took great pains not to make a sound as he approached the bush. With his Glock raised in front of his face, he pointed at the crouched figure.

"Drop the weapon and stand up real slow, hands behind your head."

CHAPTER 43

I didn't have many advantages, so I made the most of the ones I had.

I knew Crocker's energy and mental state would be low after spending the day on constant alert for my arrival. He expected me; not knowing when gave me an edge.

Dressed in black with camouflage paint on my face, I lay low in the scrub at four thirty in the morning. I brought my trusted Glock, a Ka-bar knife, and a lightweight monocular. When I packed for Broome, there wasn't a reason to bring my anti-night vision Ghillie suit. I missed the added camouflage it could have provided.

A light breeze kept me cool in the damp summer heat. The half-moon created deep shadows off the back of the house and barn. I couldn't see any details in the pitch black behind the house. I listened for any sounds that would indicate I was being hunted.

I had searched the perimeter, slow and careful, for signs Crocker might be near or had set trip wires to inform him of my arrival. There wasn't any evidence anyone had passed through this section of the woods.

Crawling to an oak, I rose to my full height, knowing low branches obscured the outline of my blackened face. I reached for the monocular. An unhurried scan of the surrounding woods didn't offer any new information.

I wondered about Crocker's game plan. If it was killing Karen, it was done; he was gone and sitting on a white sand beach. If he was setting a trap for me, then he kept her alive as bait to lure me here. In that case, the clock was ticking on Karen's life.

Karen was still alive. She had to be. I realized I *needed* her to be alive.

From this point forward, Crocker controlled the clock. The longer this situation played out, the less time I would have if I had to search elsewhere. Choosing the next thick oak, twenty feet along the perimeter, I ran. From this new viewpoint, I was in line with a door, slightly ajar, revealing the inside of the barn.

Kneeling at the base of the tree, I listened for any telltale clicks of a weapon, crackling of dry leaves, or cries for help. The only sound was the constant chatter of insects that halted when I moved and began again when I stopped. If Crocker were close, he would have taken the opportunity to kill me.

There appeared to be only two places Karen Martin could be: in the house or the barn. I wanted to check the barn first since it would afford me the opportunity to survey the house from the loft. Trying to make myself as small a target as possible by bending low, I left the cover of the trees. The door on this side of the barn had been nailed shut earlier, now the nails were removed. Was I walking into a trap? I inspected the four edges of the frame for anything out of the ordinary. It looked fine, and I was uncomfortable spending more time out in the open.

I opened the door and entered, Glock first. My mouth dry, I froze inside the doorway. A chill shook my upper body. My eyes fixed on the one yellow bulb in the center of the barn and the terrifying shadow it cast.

A figure tied to a chair, head slumped, hung from a beam ten feet in the air. Dressed in black jeans and a hooded sweatshirt, I couldn't tell if the person was dead or alive. My stomach clenched at the thought it might be Karen Martin.

CHAPTER 44

Finally!

After monitoring Holt's movements, unseen, Crocker positioned himself on the porch of the house where he could see Holt on the right side of the barn.

Crocker was borderline between anger and rage. His supply of energy bars had run out. The water was gone. He had been awake for most of the last twenty hours except for a couple of short naps. Karen Martin was fading, perhaps into a coma, but he didn't care.

The longer this goes on the greater my risk.

He watched Holt enter through the only way possible.

Crocker picked up the five-gallon can of gasoline and ran to the barn. He anticipated Holt entering from the side closest to the perimeter. The other three sides had been doused with gasoline earlier. Crocker left only two exits for Holt: the door by which he entered and the loft door. Splashing the remaining gasoline on the door, he trailed the liquid away five feet. Crocker dropped a lit match. *Whoosh.*

A line of fire sped toward the door, igniting it like dry tinder. He smiled as the flames licked up the wall and began their slow crawl around the barn.

CHAPTER 45

The twelve-inch square timber held the slack body without bowing in the center, so I hoped it would be able to handle another 210 pounds. I mounted the beam, one leg on each side. I felt a little give and knew it would get worse. Sweat broke out on my forehead. I leaned forward and shimmied toward the center.

A smell of burning wood and swirls of gray-black smoke wafted my way. That was the moment I noticed the flames darting under the door. *Shit.*

The bowing was more pronounced as I hit mid-beam. In order to untie the knot, I needed some play in the rope. I lifted the deadweight with both arms. When I had enough slack, I used my left hand to pick at the knot. Too heavy to hold for long, a few seconds later, I gently let it down.

There were large wooden pegs at foot-wide intervals along the side of the beam, thick enough to hold the weight. Once again, I heaved up the chair and its occupant until I had four feet of slack. I created three loops around a peg and lowered the chair, leaving enough rope to work with.

I could see flames advancing up the right side of the barn. Luckily, the earlier rain left the wood damp, slowing the fire. I used the point of my Ka-bar to loosen the knot. It was a slow process, and I hadn't much time. Despite the rising temperature and smoke, I worked steadily until, at last, I undid the knot.

With the fire spreading, it was now or never. Tightly gripping the rope, I unfurled the coils from the pegs and lowered the chair to the barn floor.

Lurching back to the hayloft, I descended the ship's ladder, ran to the chair, and lifted the slack head. *Maddie.*

I held her face in my hands. "Maddie!" Her eyes were taking too long to focus on me so I shouted again, "Maddie, wake up!" I cut her free and untied the rope from the chair to take with me.

She shook her head, regaining her vision and took in our situation. "Lucas. We have to get up to the loft." Maddie rose unsteadily and sat back down. She stretched her legs several times to get the blood circulating and stood again. "Let's go."

We climbed the ladder, raced to the hayloft door, and I opened it.

A shot splintered the frame.

I slammed the door shut and realized fire was creeping up the front of the barn.

"Maddie, can we get out through the cupola?"

"Yes, but then what? We'll be on the roof with a psycho waiting to pick us off while we try to get down."

"Have you a better idea?"

"No. C'mon."

A sturdy door on the opposite end of the loft hid stairs to the cupola. I went up first. Through one of the four silver grills, I spotted Crocker sitting on the porch of the house, opposite the front of the barn. He held a sniper rifle. Using the handle of my Ka-bar, I punched out a grill to exit down the back of the building. I pushed the top half of my body through and palmed the roof to pull out the rest. Maddie followed, and I took her hands and pulled her onto the roof.

We lay flat against the asphalt shingles making it difficult for Crocker to shoot. I inched over to the back of the barn and peered down. The flames were turning the corner at the base. Good enough. Crawling back to Maddie, I created a half loop from the rope and tossed it over the cupola, knotting it on our side. The length of the rope would get us halfway down. We would have to jump the last ten or so feet.

I looked over the edge once more and saw the fire had spread the entire length of the barn and up three feet where the dampness began.

"Maddie, the fire's spreading. You go first. When you get near the flames, kick-off the barn and drop down beyond it."

Without hesitation, Maddie grabbed the rope from my hands and leapt over like a descending mountain climber. I liked this woman.

She jumped to the ground, rolled, and stood, giving me a thumbs-up. The flames charged higher up the wall. Not to be outdone, I went backwards, kicking off the barn and sliding down the rope. As I reached the level of the flames, I pushed off for the last time and dropped to the ground, landing next to Maddie.

Now all we had to do was keep the barn between Crocker and us, and find a safe place to regroup. I turned and began to rise when I saw a figure looming over us.

"Holt, you are a never-ending pain in my ass." Crocker sighted down the end of his Glock and grinned.

CHAPTER 46

John Crocker stood stock-still.

He stared down the length of the Glock pointed between Maddie and me. Having enough daylight to make out his features, I studied his face. He squinted and his jaw clenched. He appeared torn, trying to weigh decisions. I glanced at the burning building. The flames had passed the damp section of the barn, devouring the wood at a fierce pace.

"Get up, Holt." Crocker's face relaxed. Whatever idea he came up with pleased him. I needed to make Crocker feel confident and in-charge. I rose to one knee, hands behind my head, and stood up.

Crocker said, "Use your left hand and throw the Glock and the Ka-bar into the woods behind you."

I did as I was told while trying to take note where the weapons landed. His next order was for me to walk six feet towards the front of the barn and halt. My back to Crocker, I paced two yards and stopped.

"Now you, Sheriff. Same drill. Stand up and get rid of the gun."

Gravel crunched as Maddie moved a couple of yards behind me. A breeze blew the thickening smoke in my direction, and I coughed to expel the toxic air from my lungs.

"Okay, Holt, move to the front of the barn...and pick up the pace. Follow him, Sheriff, but keep your distance."

I passed the barn and kept walking, my breathing slow and labored. Why didn't he just shoot us where we sat? At night, no one would notice the black smoke, but dawn was approaching. Time was not his ally.

"Stop, Holt. Sheriff, move to the edge of the woods."

I half turned. Maddie stood with her hands on the back of her head ten feet away. Crocker turned away from me and fired.

I took one step backwards from sheer shock and two forward towards Crocker. His Glock pointed at me again. Maddie was on the ground, bleeding from her right thigh. Her face twisted in agony mixed with anger. I could tell she wasn't going to give him the satisfaction of expressing pain.

My mouth was dry and my chest tightened. I had to gain control of the situation but needed an opportunity. Crocker grinned like a maniacal clown.

"It's almost light," he said. "I'm running out of time. This is how it's going to go." The clown grin remained as he released the clip from his Glock and pocketed it. Crocker removed the shell in the chamber and threw the gun twenty feet behind him. Next, he unlatched the sheath holding the Ka-bar to his lower leg and tossed it near the Glock.

"This is your chance, Holt. Look at her. The pain is terrible. You have to win fast before your girlfriend bleeds out."

We were fifteen feet apart when he began circling me. His face glazed with sweat, rivulets running between pockmarks and scars. The smart move was to kill us and run, but he was driven by his hatred of me. Still, I had to ask the question burning inside me.

"Where's Karen Martin?"

"Just like that? Okay, Holt, I'll tell you. She's in Hell."

Crocker spread his arms, hunched like a sumo wrestler, then charged.

He was taller and had a longer arm reach. I needed to outsmart him to win. I charged. His eyes gave away his surprise, but it didn't slow him down. At the last possible second, I ducked and pushed toward his waist. His momentum carried him onto my back. I stood up. He tumbled over me and crashed to the ground.

An image of a possibly dead Karen Martin flashed through my mind and anger boiled inside me. I ran to him and raised my leg to crush his head. He rolled away just in time. My heel slammed to the hard dirt, and a shock rose up my spine. I backed away a few yards on the ball of my other foot, while trying to hide the pain.

Crocker stood and took the time to dust himself off. I wondered if he was stalling—thinking about the time he had left. His eyes darted to the Ka-bar and back to me. I was between him and the knife. I glanced at Maddie. Her pain was evident. She had used her belt as a tourniquet, but she needed to get to a hospital.

Feinting a run at me, Crocker circled to my left and headed for his Ka-bar.

I tackled his legs, and he hit the ground, face down, well short of the knife. Crawling up his body, I received an elbow to the head for my effort. I rolled off and away, attempting to clear my blurred vision.

Thick, black smoke rose from the barn, contrasting the clear morning sky. Someone would call the fire department and Deputy Brimmer. I feared if Brimmer showed up and saw Maddie's condition, it might cause a knee-jerk reaction to shoot Crocker. If that happened, I might never find Karen Martin.

He moved in close, still in a wrestler's crouch. I shifted my feet in the upright stance of a boxer. I knew he meant to tackle me, and I wasn't going let that happen.

In a surprise move, he stood up and feinted a jab. I went to block it, and he grabbed my other arm, pulling me in toward him. I returned an elbow to his face and watched his bloodshot eyes roll inside his head. He staggered several steps backwards. Crocker rushed again, feinted another jab, and landed a roundhouse to my cheek. After shaking off the initial pain, I moved in and landed an uppercut to his chin. We were both bloody and trading punches, neither giving quarter.

I stepped back, covertly getting a view of Crocker's legs, then moved in again, holding his psychotic stare. I began a kick up toward his groin but instead used my right leg to sweep his left leg from under him. Again, he went down like a bag of stones. Crocker rose, but he winced and grabbed his left side.

From the corner of my eye, I could see Maddie, limp and still, the tourniquet slack on her leg. Crocker's knife and gun were behind him, and he was in front of me. Would he quickly hobble away, leaving me to help Maddie? Would he make another run for the Ka-bar?

He quick-turned and limped rapidly toward the knife. I had to make up ten feet between us and did. I dived low and hard and reached the Ka-bar first. Crocker landed on top of me, knees crunching my back, and grabbed my hand with both of his, lifting and twisting. To counter the pressure, I stiffened my wrist. Crocker's knees gouged ruts in my back. Inhaling deeply, I ignored the pain and focused on freeing my right arm from beneath me. Pushing up with my trapped arm, I jerked it free. Able to rock my body, Crocker tumbled off me and onto his back. He had no choice but to pull me along to maintain a hold on the Ka-bar. My back on his chest and Crocker attempting to break my wrist, I had one move I hoped would work. I slid to the left and, as hard as possible, I rammed my right elbow into his solar plexus. With the air knocked from his lungs, Crocker turned his focus to breathing and I yanked my wrist free. I spun and faced him with the knife to his throat.

It wasn't until that moment I decided Crocker's fate. I knew it would only end one way.

I can't spend the rest of my life looking over my

shoulder.

His eyes told me he knew it too.

For Karen Martin. For Mary Wells. For Maddie.

I plunged the knife into his chest. His eyes bulged. He tried to take a breath, but the air hole in his collapsed lung wouldn't permit it.

I shifted the weight of my body onto the Ka-bar and sunk it to the hilt.

Chapter 47

Emergency responders arrived and began to work on the blazing barn and Maddie's gunshot wound. Cars of locals lined Farm Road. I watched as Alex Clancy examined Crocker's body. He saw me. I must have looked as if I needed verification that the knife I plunged into the madman's chest did its job.

"He's dead," Clancy stated, making it official. He rose and gave the order to bag the corpse and have it brought to the morgue. He half smiled at me. "Business sure has picked up since you came to town, Mr. Holt."

It wasn't funny, and a left-handed compliment to be sure.

Deputy Brimmer stood over Maddie, who lay on an ambulance gurney. As I walked over to the sheriff, he moved away to control the crowd congregating at the lane to the farm.

"Maddie?"

Her eyes opened partially, then wider. She tried to rise then winced in pain and lay down again.

"What? You want me to say you're my hero? Forget it."

I smiled. "Time enough for that later. Crocker is dead. We still don't know where Karen is. She has to be on this property somewhere."

Maddie struggled to speak. "Lucas, I tried. I tried to find her." She paused and took a deep breath. "He found me...before I could."

"I know, Maddie. We all tried. We'll find her. Just rest."

Maddie shook her head and tugged hard on my sleeve. I leaned in close.

"I remembered. There's a root cellar." She raised a shaky hand and pointed to an area on the right side of the house. "Find it."

I yelled to Brimmer. He and Delaney followed me. We trudged through the dead leaves, branches, and brush covering the ground. Spreading out, we began clearing the area with leg sweeps. I pounded the dirt every few feet, hoping to discover a void under the surface.

Fifteen minutes later, I heard hollowness in response to my tamping. Brushing aside the scrub, I found a trap door, camouflaged with dirt and sprigs of leaves. A thought wormed its way into my consciousness and halted me in my tracks. *Wait. A trap. Was Crocker's plan, I kill Karen Martin and myself by opening the cellar door?*

Brimmer was as anxious and stressed as I was. "C'mon, Holt. What are you waiting for?"

I gave them the time-honored, time-out signal by putting my hands together in the form of the letter "T." *Crocker made this personal. He'd have a backup plan.*

I walked full circle around the door to the root cellar but didn't find anything out of the ordinary. I glanced up. Brimmer and Delaney got the message and took a few steps back. Maddie sat up straight on the gurney staring at me, and I sensed apprehension from her posture. Doc Clancy strode with purpose in our direction.

As a Delta Force operative, Crocker was trained in explosives and booby traps. I searched the ground until I found a stone two inches high. Lying on the ground next to the cellar, I gently lifted the door and propped it up with the stone.

"Brimmer, hand me your pocket flashlight." I shone the bright LED light in a slow motion along the underside perimeter of the door. It only took a moment to find the wire attached to the right corner of the door and follow it down between the steps. I recognized the shape.

"What do you see?" Brimmer asked.

"A grenade." Crocker had used the steps to anchor the grenade so when the door opened, it would pull the pin. Raising the cellar door as little as a few more inches would have ended me—and anyone in the cellar.

"Karen," I called, shining the light around the dark cellar. No response. In one corner on the wall, I saw a shadow cast by what could have been a body. It didn't move. *Shit.* I had no choice but to open the door without setting off the grenade.

I stood. "Delaney, ask the EMTs for the strongest pair of scissors they have."

He nodded and hurried away. I liked him. He

didn't ask questions.

Delaney returned with the scissors. "Holt, everyone is asking for an update. Especially Maddie…who insists I find out what's going on."

"She's going to have to wait a few minutes." I lay down again and slid one hand under the door. Able to reach in just past my wrist, it was enough space to pinch the wire between my thumb and forefinger. I inserted the blades of the scissors through the opening and above my left hand. I paused, took a deep breath, and snipped the wire. So far so good. I eased the grenade a few inches to the dirt floor, rose, and lifted the cellar door.

The quiet outside was almost as deafening as the silence coming from the root cellar. I looked for another grenade, C-4, or any other potential traps. The daylight penetrated to the bottom of the cellar. I slowly descended, avoiding the step shielding the grenade. In the dirt was a maze of footprints of large heavy boots with deep treads. A balled-up object covered with a blanket lay still against one wall. The air was fetid. Something had died in that cellar. My jaw clamped shut, and I took short shallow breaths through my nose.

She's alive. She has to be.

"Karen," I shouted as my heart hammered in my chest. Dropping to the floor, I yanked the blanket away. I recoiled at the sight, but it wasn't human.

Karen Martin wasn't there.

CHAPTER 48

The fact that Karen Martin wasn't in the root cellar spread to the many spectators on Farm Road. I watched concerned, optimistic faces drop with disappointment at the news. Two teary teenage girls held hands for comfort. No one left despite the threat of rain.

I recognized two people in the crowd: the Martins. The last few days left them looking pale and haggard. I wished I had good news. I'd been where they were, and my heart ached for them.

Thunder cracked as dark clouds gathered in the distance. Restless, Brimmer and the other deputies milled around, not sure what to do next. Alex Clancy remained for the moment when we found Karen Martin. I walked back to Maddie who still rested on the gurney.

"Don't you think you should be on your way to the hospital?"

"Not yet," she said. "The bleeding stopped and the I.V. is helping. I'm weak and need to rest, but I can do that here. Lucas, I was sure she was there.

Where else could she be?"

"Good question."

We were out of possibilities, and it was my fault. There were ways I could've subdued Crocker but didn't. When he told me Karen Martin was in hell, my mind went down a tortured road where I pictured her lying in the woods, her body twisted, bent and bloody. Then Maddie fell unconscious from Crocker's gunshot, and I feared she was gone. My thoughts ran down another dark road, one where I repeatedly stabbed Crocker's arms, legs, and pockmarked face. A dog with a spiked collar pulled at a chain I held, wanting to shred Crocker's throat.

Peter Delaney stood near the ambulance. "Peter, what about those search dogs? We could use them now."

"They're supposed to arrive this morning. Let me check." Delaney made a phone call. "They're twenty minutes away. I'll tell them to come straight here."

I returned to the root cellar, hoping to find something of Karen's which we could use to put the dogs onto her scent. Repulsed, I searched what Crocker left behind in the blanket. There was nothing I could use. It was possible that at one time Karen had been wrapped in the blanket, but it was now compromised. Moving to the few shelves, I knelt on the ground, feeling the cool dampness on my knees, and used the flashlight to look under them…and there it was. A black sweatband, like runners wear on their forehead. It was fairly clean so I knew it hadn't been there long. I left the cellar and headed toward the Martins.

As I verified with Sarah Martin that Karen owned a band like the one I found, a white van pulled onto the lane. A man jumped out, rounded the back of it, and opened the doors. Out shot two excited dogs, barking and pacing in circles around their handler. I ran to the van and Delaney introduced us.

"Lucas Holt, this is Henry McCoy. He's been training search dogs for ten years." He put his hand out, and I grasped it. McCoy had an engaging smile and an easy way about him.

"Good to meet you, Lucas. Hope we can be of some help."

"I'm counting on it. I found a sweatband I believe belongs to a kidnap victim. I'm guessing she isn't far from here, and I hope she's alive."

McCoy's face turned somber. "Well, I hope so too. But we'll find her either way."

I handed him the sweatband and watched as the excited canines sniffed it, danced around as if they were about to play their favorite game, and put their noses to the ground.

When we found Karen, she would likely need medical attention. Walking past Maddie, I could see her arguing with Doc Clancy. From what I overheard, she didn't want to leave for the hospital, and he was having none of it. Two attendants lifted the gurney, slid it in the back of the ambulance, and climbed in. She saw me.

"Lucas, call me as soon as you know something." I nodded and waved.

"Clancy, coming?" I asked.

"Try and keep me away."

"We're coming too," Brimmer spoke for himself and Delaney.

We followed McCoy and the dogs.

***

With their tails whipping back and forth, the dogs, a German shepherd named Nine and a white Lab named Eleven, caught and tracked the scent north past the barn. Both tugged hard, pulling McCoy toward the woods as they alternated between sniffs and pants. I hoped Karen was close and that Nine and Eleven would go straight to her. We didn't have much time and I wasn't sure how effective the dogs would be if it began to pour rain. If we didn't find her, all that was left was to take a shotgun approach to the problem and get as many people as possible, spread them out, and hope someone stumbled on her. With rain coming, that seemed like a very low probability solution.

Ten minutes out, what I feared most happened—the dogs lost the scent. Their noses still to the ground, Nine and Eleven separated, pushing outward in different directions. My chest tightened. There weren't any homes or farms in this area, which meant that Crocker dumped Karen. He either left her unprotected against the weather or hidden by bushes and trees. In that case, the more time that passed, the less likely we would find her alive.

Nine looked up at his handler and let out a soft whimper. Eleven's tail rose and he pulled east, toward a denser area of trees. He wasn't excited, but he was firm about the direction. Nine picked up the scent too and we were off again.

We'd been in the woods nearly an hour when McCoy spoke, "We're close. Eleven seems committed. I'm going to let him loose. I'm not worried about him getting too far ahead of us because Nine will find him."

The Labrador ran in a northeasterly direction and quickly disappeared from sight. McCoy and I trotted along behind the Shepherd while Brimmer, Delaney, and Clancy pulled up the rear. After five minutes, the two deputies paused. The rest of us continued our fast pace.

Another ten minutes passed and it began to drizzle. As I prayed that we'd find her before we were caught in a deluge of rain, we heard Eleven's faint barks. My breathing became deep and rapid.

She's alive. She has to be.

Rushing to catch up to the dog, we stopped when Eleven trotted out from behind tall junipers and then disappeared again. The dog paced back and forth as if trying to decide if he should run to his master or stay where he was. The closer we got to the dog, the more he barked. Thinking it was a good sign, I ran ahead of the others, praying it was finally over. Praying for a positive end.

When I approached, Eleven moved to sniff my clothes and then turned back to the result of his search. I ran past some shrubs and a large mound of dirt and stood at the edge of a deep hole—the size of a grave. It was empty.

From his vantage point to the left of me, McCoy tried to call Eleven away, but the dog continued to pace and bark. A few feet from the dugout grave was another mound of dirt. I stepped closer and my breath caught when I saw the partially concealed body of Karen Martin.

Down two feet from the ground and buried in dirt from her neck to her feet, Karen's pale face protruded from the soil. Her eyes were closed, her mouth covered with duct tape. McCoy shouted to the others as I jumped into the hole and straddled the mound covering her. I scooped out handfuls of dirt from around her head and chest. Pelts of rain came down hard, but were buffeted by the trees. Hundreds of worms crawled through the damp, loose dirt framing her body. Dread replaced shock when I removed the tape and couldn't feel her breath. Grabbing her shoulders, I lifted Karen to free her chest from the grave. I held her in my arms and checked for her pulse. I exhaled in relief. Her pulse was weak, but steady.

She's alive. Thank God.

Doc Clancy leaned over, black bag in hand. "Alive?"

I smiled as the knots in my shoulders relaxed and my stress melted away. The search was over. "Yes."

"Well, get out of that damn hole and let me do my job."

CHAPTER 49

Waiting until I knew Karen Martin's prognosis, giving myself time to regroup and collect my thoughts, it was a few days after the rescue when I called Janet Maxwell.

"Mr. Holt, I've been impatient to hear from you. Please tell me you've found her."

"I have," I said, my voice reflecting an unspoken "but" at the end.

"And? Where is she for God's sake? Don't keep me in suspense. It's what I'm paying you a lot of money to tell me."

I dreaded the phone call and having to tell her she couldn't know where her daughter was yet. I thought some things were better said in person.

"Mrs. Maxwell, there were some unforeseen events, and while your daughter is alive, she's been through an ordeal."

She asked rather nonchalantly, "An ordeal? What's happened?"

"I can't go into that right now. I'll come and see you when I get back to New York. You have to keep in mind your daughter is still a minor. You'll have to wait a few months to make contact."

That news received more reaction.

"Months? Absolutely not. I demand to know where she is right now. It's what I'm paying you for!"

"I know, but a few months—"

"In a few months it will be too late!" Her shrill voice pierced my ears, and I held the phone away from my head for a moment.

"Too late for what? You've already waited seventeen years. A few months will—"

"Will ruin everything. I'll sue you for breach of contract. Expect to hear from Brown and Harrington in the future."

With that, she disconnected. I stood staring at the phone, rerunning the conversation through my mind. I had expected her to be disappointed, but she was more enraged than let down. I wasn't sure what to make of it. I thought she needed time to adjust to the news and be in a calmer state when I saw her in New York.

***

I entered Memorial Medical Center and into a blast of icy air, set to freeze out any humidity and more than a few germs. I shivered but not from the cold. Hospitals aren't my favorite places. Most of my experience with them has been dire, except when Marnie was born. That was a long time ago. Since then, I've watched both my parents wither away from terminal illnesses no amount of medical and technological advancement could cure.

Shaking off the bout of morbidity, I focused on the reason I was there. Karen Martin was stable and expected to make a complete physical recovery as soon as all the drugs left her system. She would have to undergo a psychiatric evaluation before being released, but her positive response to the rescue was a good sign.

Taking the elevator to the second floor, I thought about what I would say to the Martins when I saw them. They had been cold toward me, blaming me for Karen's abduction. Of course, I wasn't directly responsible, but I understood. Still, I didn't like being on the receiving end of their anger. At least this case had a happy ending—of a sort. Although beyond my control, the death of Mary Wells weighed heavily on my mind. The Martins stood outside Karen's room when I approached.

"She's asleep," Sarah Martin said in a rather brisk tone.

"How's she doing?" I asked.

Daniel Martin looked at me as if I'd asked the world's stupidest question. He seemed to hold back some nasty reply. Instead he said, "Quite well, considering she was plied with enough drugs to put her in a permanent coma."

I glanced past the Martins through the open door. Karen lay in a semi-upright position, her eyes closed. Searching for words, the best I could come up with was, "She seems to be resting comfortably."

They both turned to look at their daughter and then back at me. I interpreted their faces as saying, "No thanks to you." I took a deep breath and changed the subject.

"Would you like to get a cup of coffee? If you wouldn't mind, I'd like to speak with you."

Daniel Martin's eyes caught his wife's and held them a few seconds. He must have read her assent and relief. He nodded. As long as I was there, they wouldn't leave Karen's side. "We could use a coffee."

The hospital cafeteria was crowded, but we found a table, sat, and sipped our drinks. The Martins made a handsome couple. I hadn't noticed before how attractive Sarah Martin was. Her face, framed by chin-length, thick hair, was no longer drawn and tear-stained. With high cheekbones and a healthy complexion, she was as fit as her husband.

Sarah grasped her cup in one hand while the other rested on the table, content in her husband's strong grip. Karen Martin was a very lucky young woman.

Daniel Martin broke the silence. "Mr. Holt, now that you've found our daughter, what will you tell your client?"

Martin's words were clear and perfectly chosen. They were Karen's parents; Janet Maxwell was not.

"I'll be honest with you. I took this case because my client gave me the impression Karen might be in some danger." I hesitated a split second too long.

"She wasn't until you began to search for her," Martin said, and I watched his jaw clench and the grasp on his wife's hand tighten.

I didn't want to make excuses or try to lessen their anger by telling them about Marnie and my determination to unite children with their parents. I only had Janet Maxwell's word that she made the decision to give up her child under duress. I was also bound to a verbal contract with my client to find her daughter and would have to report my findings, with one exception.

"Since Karen is still a minor, I've decided to withhold her location until she reaches the age of majority. You might consider telling Karen about her adoption before then."

Sarah Martin's eyes glazed with tears. "That doesn't give us much time to explain why we've kept it a secret and for her to forgive us. Karen will want to know everything about her mother and father." Sarah swiped a drop from her cheek. "And you know she'll want to see them—to know them."

I knew. Although I believed every parent should have the right to raise their own children, I knew what they were thinking. Daniel and Sarah gave Karen a secure and loving home. After witnessing the family's reunion when Karen was rescued, I knew Karen loved her parents with all her heart. And I also knew the Martins' feared losing part of that heart if and when Karen connected with her birth parents.

I wanted to apologize, but instead said, "I know it's a difficult situation. I wish you all the best."

***

My next stop was the fourth floor. Sheriff Grange was awaiting my arrival after insisting the doctor discharge her. I've endured gunshot wounds and thought the sheriff was not giving herself enough time to heal. I had told her as much. The stubborn woman refused to hear me.

But as soon as I stepped off the elevator, I could hear her.

Maddie sat in a wheelchair next to the nurses' station, speaking loudly into her cell phone.

"I'm breaking out of here today. I should be—wait, here's my ride now. Be ready to fill me in on any new developments later this afternoon."

I smiled and waved to her. She acknowledged me as she disconnected the call and signaled the orderly she was ready. He handed the sheriff a plastic bag that contained some personal items. She said, "Let's go," and he wheeled her down the corridor toward me.

"How did I know you'd be in a hurry?" I asked.

"If you knew I'd be in a hurry, why are you late?" I saw the slight upturned corners of her mouth. Not quite a smile, but it was promising.

I took the bag from her lap in a gesture of gallantry before she could object. When the elevator opened, I held the door and bowed as she passed me.

"Knock it off," she said, but I could hear the amusement in her voice.

The orderly helped Maddie into the front passenger seat of the Rover parked out front. After she was strapped and settled, I quipped, "Where to, madam?"

I expected some sarcastic retort. Instead, she stared ahead for what seemed like an endless few seconds. I began to feel I was right that she left the hospital too soon. She turned to me. Her forehead creased with lines and she bit her lip. She took a long time to answer a simple question. I could take her to one of two places, her office, or home. Her decision surprised me.

"Lucas, would you mind taking me to the farm?"

CHAPTER 50

The air smelled of rain-washed grass and burnt cedar.

We sat in the car on the clearing between the house and what was left of the barn. Fire trucks from two neighboring towns had assisted Broome firefighters in controlling the fire. The main concern was protecting the surrounding woods. A compact gravel path that ran around the barn slowed its spread, and a summer deluge of rain snuffed out any stubborn embers.

Maddie stared a moment at the pile of charred siding and then turned her attention to the house.

"I lived there," she said, "in that house—in that hideous pink room. It wasn't bad when my grandmother was alive. We moved in with her when my father lost his job. He hated having to take charity and drank heavily. My mother died when I was five and my grandmother two years later. It was me and Dad in the house and him still with no job." Maddie paused and leaned against the headrest.

"It must have been hard, but I'm sure your father

did his best," I said.

She shook her head. "He didn't know what to do with me. I'd been homeschooled by a friend of my mother. My father didn't want me to be with the other kids at school. I guess he was afraid of what I might say that would embarrass him."

"Men do have their pride," I said in her father's defense.

She let out a joyless laugh, full of scorn and contempt. "It was ludicrous that he had so much pride. He was a selfish bastard. When my father could no longer pay my tutor, he sent me to my mother's sister in Ohio. It's where I was born. I didn't intend ever to come back."

I hadn't known Maddie Grange long, and it had been a rough week for both of us. She had suffered with a gunshot wound and I with self-recriminations for, perhaps, taking the case for selfish reasons and putting Karen Martin in harm's way. I found it strangely comforting to have Maddie open up to me.

"So you came back to be with him. That took courage. It's admirable."

Maddie shook her head and chuckled a low throaty laugh. "No. It wasn't courageous at all. At first, I refused to see him."

"What's important is that you did," I said, thinking she was being hard on herself. "You gave your father his dying wish."

"No, Lucas. I didn't give a rat's ass about my drunken father's wishes."

She seemed to want to say more so I remained quiet.

"I worked undercover in Baltimore. My cover was blown, and my life was in danger. I left and had nowhere else to go. My aunt had no children, and when she died, she left her house to me. Since I couldn't go back there, I sold it and came here."

I wanted to know more about her undercover work in Baltimore but would wait for a better time. She swallowed hard and turned away from me. I caught her swiping a tear before it ran down her cheek.

"What will you do now? Sell this property too?"

Maddie tilted her head toward me. "No, I think I'll restore it. I have pictures of the house from when my grandparents lived there. If I go back far enough, the memories are pretty nice."

"Really? You'd keep everything the same?" After what she told me, I was surprised. "It's one way to deal with your demons."

"Yeah, but I'd change one thing."

"What's that?"

Maddie gave me the same beautiful smile she'd given someone at the Grog and Hog.

"I'd repaint that hideous pink room."

***

I drove the sheriff back to her cabin, pulling as close to the building as possible. It was diminutive and serene. I thought about how scaling down to a few belongings and living more simply could be cathartic. But I like my brownstone *and* my stuff. Without all of it, it would be my demons and me. That wouldn't be liberating—it'd be hell.

Maddie shifted in her seat, and I figured she was anxious to leave me and go inside. I turned off the car. Before I could open the door, she touched my arm and asked, "Who is Sheila Rand?"

She held the Rand file in her hand, and as I began to talk about the cold case, she flipped through the report and photos. When I told her about Marnie's kidnapping and why I took the Maxwell case, Maddie listened with the consideration of a therapist. Besides Scully, I hadn't discussed the Rand case or its effect on my life with anyone else.

"So now you're not sure Grayson killed this woman?" she asked when I finished speaking.

"To be honest, I wasn't even sure at the time. We couldn't verify his alibi and the witness was too convenient and unreliable. I believed, if not Grayson, someone connected with him."

"What about the lawyer you mentioned? What's his name? Cain?"

"He was most likely the one who persuaded my captain to lay off Grayson, but there was no evidence connecting him to the murder."

"What about a motive? If this was a professional hit ordered by someone to protect Grayson, it's a sloppy job. Did you think it was a crime of passion on Grayson's part? Had she threatened him or was she blackmailing him?" Maddie asked all the same questions I'd asked myself.

"Again, no evidence to suggest that."

"Did you consider this was a random act by one of Rand's clients? She was in the business, after all."

"Sure, we did. There were no prints other than the victim and Grayson's. We knew he'd been to her apartment—couldn't prove it was on that night, though."

Maddie stared at the close up of Sheila Rand, her hair matted with blood, her earlobe torn. She didn't look at me when she spoke. "You must have hundreds of unsolved cold cases. We had as many in Baltimore. Some you can never solve no matter how thorough an investigation. It's even affected your decision for taking the case involving Karen Martin. Sometimes, Lucas, you have to let it go."

A jolt of terror spread through me at the thought of letting go of the Rand case. That was akin to letting go of the effort to find my daughter. Maddie sensed my struggle.

"You do what you have to, Lucas. Right now, I have to get inside and rest. I'm feeling a lot more tired than I thought I would. Lucas, I want to..." Maddie paused, lowered her eyes, and then raised them to fix on mine. "Thank you for saving my life."

She was sincere, and I surprised myself by not blurting out a flippant retort. I knew it was hard for her to express her emotions and was glad to have been the recipient. Although I'd never say it aloud to Maddie, she made me feel like her knight in shining armor. To some extent, we had just bared our souls to each other. I'd not done that in a long time.

Maddie didn't flinch when I raised my hand to brush her cheek with the back of my fingers. Pushing her hair away, I cupped the back of her head and drew it toward me, placing my lips over hers for a soft, gentle kiss. After a searing moment, I broke the kiss, and still holding her head, said, "You're welcome."

"Hmm, I might have to let you save me more often."

"Anytime. I released my hold, and we both smiled and readied to exit the car.

Maddie glanced once more at Sheila Rand before slipping the photo back in the folder. "Beautiful earring. Looks expensive."

"Yeah, one was missing. We never found it. We tried to trace them to a jeweler but no luck. We think the killer took it as a trophy."

"Then the killer is definitely not a female." Maddie grinned. "A woman would have taken both."

CHAPTER 51

As I'd hoped, the next time I spoke with Janet Maxwell, she was pleasant.

No longer threatening lawsuits, she invited me to her apartment so I could tell her all about her daughter. I cringed at the word "all" and mentally prepared for the encounter. I resolved to give the Martins time to explain the circumstances to Karen and planned to stick to my guns.

Parsing the conversation with Maxwell when I had called her from Broome, I was again struck by her reaction. Why would a few more months be too late? Did it have something to do with Grayson and the election? Then it hit me. She had used me as a tool to get even with Todd Grayson.

"Hell hath no fury…"

***

I arrived at Maxwell's uptown apartment just after seven in the evening. In my search for a place to live in Manhattan, I learned a bit of the history of its residences. Maxwell's 1930s building was, at one time, home to the likes of John D. Rockefeller, Jr. and Jackie Kennedy Bouvier. Nice digs, but a little too blue blood for me.

Maxwell came to the door looking regal and svelte in a white jumpsuit with, I couldn't help but notice, a plunging V that dipped to her waist. A sapphire jewel around her neck mirrored her eyes. She'd swept her hair up into some kind of twist. If nothing else, Janet Maxwell was a stunning woman. Had she meant to seduce me into telling her where her daughter was?

"Mr. Holt, please come in. Can I get you something to drink? Bourbon? Wine?" She ran her eyes over my sport jacket, black tee, and jeans. "A beer, perhaps?"

"Nothing for me, thanks, Mrs. Maxwell. I won't take up too much of your time. You appear to be dressed to go out."

She smiled brilliantly. "Please call me Janet," she said and took my arm, leading me to the sofa. "Sit. I'm going to get myself a glass of wine. Then we'll talk."

I watched her glide to a small bar cart and pour herself a drink. She sat next to me on the sofa, rested her back against the rolled arm, and crossed her long legs. Her strappy silver shoes exposed narrow, pedicured feet and pale pink polished toes, which hovered perilously close to my knee. I shifted to avoid touching her.

"So—may I call you Lucas?" I must have moved my head a millimeter, which she took as my assent and continued. "Lucas, have you had time to reconsider your refusal to tell me where my daughter is? You must see it's a breach of our contract not to do so. How about a compromise? Tell me where she is, and I promise not to contact her until she is eighteen."

I almost laughed. She might not contact Karen, but I was sure she'd find some way to leak the girl's location—and the bit about her birth parents to an interested third party.

"I'm sorry, Janet. I can't do that. I may not have thought about all the ramifications of this case when I first agreed to take it. You must understand—"

"No, you must understand. I *need* to know where she is. I've waited long enough. It's been hell all these years not knowing her, wondering what type of person she's become. Who does she look like? She must have changed even in the last couple of years."

Although persistent, I detected anguish in her plea. "She's a bit of both of you. But she has your eyes and nose. She's a lovely young woman."

Maxwell drained her wine. "I suppose those people who raised her did an adequate job."

"Yes, they did. You should be very grateful." Too late, I realized that was the wrong thing to say.

"Grateful?" Maxwell sprang from her seat and began to pace and rail. "I should be *grateful* to have had my child ripped from my breast and given away? I should be *grateful* that Cain saved me from a life branded as an adulterer with an illegitimate child?"

I half rose from the sofa when she moved in front of me. Her eyes bore into mine. I fell back into the seat again. Better to stay quiet and let her get it off her chest.

"Todd Grayson loved me. Really loved me. I could tell. He said he would leave his wife—said we'd make a better team for his political career. We were alike in so many ways. He just needed the right incentive. A push." She sat in the chair across from me, staring past me.

"The child should have persuaded him." Tears streamed down her face. "We should have been together, but instead he abandoned me. I couldn't believe it—thought Douglas had something to do with it. I went to him and begged him to let me see Todd. I knew once he saw me again—saw his daughter—everything would be all right."

She paused briefly before pressing on. "Instead Cain forced me to give up my baby and paid me like a common whore for my trouble. I began to think that perhaps Todd suffered too—suffered through a loveless marriage, suffered because we were apart. Cain gave him no choice. His career was too important. I accepted it—all of it—until he took up with that call girl."

Her voice filled with derision, she said the name, "Sheila Rand."

Janet Maxwell leaned back in the chair. I watched her face harden at the thought of Grayson with another woman. Her jaw clenched. I saw the venom, the hate. How had she known about Grayson's relationship with Rand? It was more than a year after she'd given up Karen. Had she really moved on? Accepted it, as she said? I made an attempt at consolation.

"That was a long time ago, Janet. You've moved on—"

"Moved on? Knowing he was cheating on his wife with another woman when he could have been with me? He moved on, hadn't he? The son-of-a bitch even gave her my jewelry. He hadn't suffered at all. Where's the justice in that? He deserves to suffer. She deserved what she got."

Maxwell smiled, and it was then I noticed the way she fondled the stone at her neck. The same way she did when I first met her—when she first mentioned Grayson's relationship with Rand. I recognized the blue teardrop. I'd seen it so many times.

The same sapphire stone that hung on Maxwell's neck had hung in Sheila Rand's torn ear.

CHAPTER 52

Janet Maxwell had murdered Sheila Rand.

That was not the only revelation to surface. Even though Todd Grayson was innocent of the crime, his handlers made sure nothing tied him to the incident. Especially the actions of a former lover, who also happened to be the mother of his illegitimate daughter. Did Douglas Cain know Maxwell had killed Rand?

The relationship between Grayson and Maxwell was one of the New York elite's best-kept secrets. In hindsight, I realized Cain *had* to shut down any investigation of Rand's death. Unsubstantiated rumors of Grayson's possible dalliance with a call girl were nothing compared to the exposure of his affair with Maxwell. Janet Maxwell had never forgiven Grayson for abandoning her, and she would have her revenge. Even if it meant using her own daughter as the means to his personal and political end.

I should have trusted my instincts, which told me to pass on the case, in spite of Maxwell's offer to give me information tying Grayson to Rand. But the proposition was too tempting. If I had something on Grayson, I'd hoped I could persuade him or his lawyer to shed some light on what happened to Marnie. In my gut, I knew they were connected.

There was no doubt in my mind what I had to do.

I rose from the sofa and slipped past Janet, who remained in the chair, her eyes staring ahead, the evidence linking her to murder clutched in her hand. I poured myself a finger's worth of her top-shelf whiskey and knocked it down in one gulp.

Fortified, I returned to sit opposite the woman who stabbed Sheila Rand to death in cold blood. I scooted forward, clasped my hands, and rested both arms in my lap. "Janet—"

Her head jerked toward me and the coolness in her eyes sent a jolt of frost up my spine.

"You know," she whispered, "don't you?"

"I know you've been deeply hurt, and you did something I'm sure you regret—"

"I have no regrets," she said and left the chair to pace again. "At least not about anything I've done of my own accord. My only regret would be not seeing Todd Grayson as miserable as he's made me."

Maxwell stood by a chest and picked up a photograph. I rose and moved closer to scan the framed photos. The one she held was of a younger Janet and a handsome gentleman who I recognized as Grayson. All the others were of both of them or just Grayson. That alarmed me. Where were the photos of her husband and son? Had she completely regressed back twenty years? She was delusional. I knew how dangerous she could be, and I had to tread carefully.

Janet whirled around and threw the picture frame across the room, shattering the glass. She pressed her palms into her temples and the tendons on her neck bulged. Before I could stop her, she ran and dropped to the floor. Shoving the shards in all directions, she tore the picture out of the frame. Blood dripped from her hand as she ripped the photograph into smaller and smaller pieces, chanting, "This is all your fault...all your...fault...all...your...fault."

She'd lost control. I pulled out my cellphone to call Scully.

Janet shouted, "What are you doing?"

I dropped the phone back in my pocket. "Janet, your hand is bleeding. Let me look at it."

"No. Stay away from me."

"It's over, Janet. I have a friend who can help. I need to call him."

"It doesn't matter who you call. Nothing you do can harm me now—it will only harm Todd. I've made sure, whether I'm here to see it or not, he will suffer. I *will* ruin him."

"Think about what it will do to your daughter."

She shook her head and sidestepped to a desk. As she opened a drawer, I pulled my .38 Special from inside my jacket and held it at my side. Janet removed a cloth from the desk and wrapped her hand. I relaxed.

"I have thought about her—every day of my life for the past seventeen years. Every day I thought about how she would help me bring down her father."

"Janet, you would use your own child as a means for revenge?"

"Don't look so surprised, Mr. Holt." The corners of her mouth rose in a sneer. "She was conceived as a means—but that didn't work. Now her existence will serve another purpose."

I'd never met a more cold and calculating woman. *If she were hungry, this woman would eat her young. Why didn't I see it?*

Maxwell was deranged. I had to get her into custody. I inched a few steps toward her. She saw my movement and the gun in my hand.

"Janet, I want you to sit back in the chair. I'm going to call Detective Scully."

"Give up? Oh no. I won't do that," she said and leaned against the desk, tucking back loose tendrils of her hair. "Lucas, I can help you, if you help me."

Her voice was no longer strained and shrill, but smooth and businesslike. I kept direct eye contact to distract her from what my hands and feet were doing.

"It's a little late for deals, Janet."

"Not for this one. You'll want to hear what I have to say. But first, put that silly gun away."

Instead, I held the gun higher. "Enough of the games, Ja—"

"Games? Locating Marnie is a game I think you'd find worth playing."

My breath caught in my throat and my anger seethed. "You will *not* use my daughter as a means to get away with murder." I yanked out my phone.

"Wait! If you don't believe me, ask Douglas,"

she said, her eyes wide and imploring.

I froze. For the first time since I met Janet Maxwell, I thought she might be telling the truth. My stance wavered, and I flushed with heat. I couldn't speak. She watched with pleasure as I processed what she implied.

I choked out the words, "No deal, Janet." I raised my .38 and stepped forward.

She gave me a chilling smile as she reached back in the desk draw and pulled out a revolver. *Shit.*

She slipped away from the desk toward the foyer, waving her weapon in front of her. Where did she think she would go? Her eyes grew with frenzy and blinked in rapid succession. Her breathing became gasps for air. Deranged and desperate—a lethal combination.

She spoke fast, her words running together, and slurred. "I know you don't want to kill me, Lucas. You want to know what happened to Marnie. I can tell you."

"Put the gun down, Janet. There's nowhere for you to go."

She laughed. "You're a self-righteous son-of-a-bitch. You would rather see me in prison than know where your daughter is. Don't be a fool. Let me go."

I couldn't let her go. How did I know if she'd give me any information after she was gone? She had to be bluffing. I shook my head, no.

Janet backed up to the elevator and pressed the button. I had less than thirty seconds until the car reached us from the lobby.

"You have three seconds to put the gun down,

Janet, or I *will* shoot you."

I sounded like I meant it. She lowered the gun and squatted to rest the weapon on the floor. "Okay, Lucas, but it's your loss."

The tension in my shoulders calmed. "You've made the right choice, Janet."

Halting at the sound of my voice, her grip still on the gun, she narrowed her eyes. Maxwell's hand flew up, her gun pointed at me.

We both fired.

The bullet from her gun missed my shoulder. My shot, meant for the arm that held her weapon, hit her in the chest when she twisted as the elevator's ding announced its arrival. She stumbled back into it. The doors closed. I ran and slammed the button to open them.

Janet Maxwell slumped on the floor, blood soaking the pure-white silk of her clothes. Raising her eyes to me, she smiled—a sad, sympathetic smile, as though she pitied me for shooting her. She inhaled a ragged last breath, grasped the sapphire gem at her throat, and closed her eyes.

CHAPTER 53

Weeks later, I sat across from Douglas Cain in his office, determined not to leap over the desk and choke the life out of him.

It was an overwhelming struggle, as I had no doubt of his guilt and responsibility for the death of Mary Wells and Ronald Glick and the kidnapping of Karen Martin. More than that was Janet Maxwell's taunt that she could help me find Marnie. She knew I didn't believe it and had suggested I ask Douglas.

Cain leaned forward with his hands clasped on his desk and cleared his throat.

"What can I do for you, Mr. Holt?"

He had a smooth baritone voice and sounded unconcerned, which grated on my nerves. His body language told a different story. I watched him shift in his seat and straighten files on his desk that were already in neat piles.

"I'm trying to tie up a few loose ends to a recent case of mine. My client was someone you knew. Janet Maxwell."

Cain had the gall to pretend to search his mind for her name. I flexed my fists open and closed, inhaling and exhaling to remain calm. The lawyer also knew how to read body language and wasted no more time with theatrics.

"Yes, yes. I knew Mrs. Maxwell—and her husband too, of course. Such a tragedy. Now the whole family is gone."

Is he kidding?

"Mr. Cain, I'm sure you know the details of Janet Maxwell's death so let's cut through the bullshit."

He recoiled at my language. Another act, I was sure. He said nothing, so I did.

"Counselor, you know I believe there's a connection between you and John Crocker." At the mention of the mercenary's name, Cain blanched. "Crocker didn't mention he and I had a history?" The lawyer breathed in short measured spurts, and I could almost hear his heart pound. *Good.* "I believe you hired him *and* Glick to stop me from finding Maxwell's daughter. In the process, Crocker murdered Mary Wells and Ronald Glick. That makes you a murderer too."

Cain tried nonchalantly to catch his breath. He began to tidy his desk again. Then he responded with the same defensive cliché that you hear all guilty parties utter in every murder mystery on TV.

"You can't prove any of that."

I ignored it, staring at him for a moment as he leaned back, crossing and uncrossing his legs. He was right. I couldn't prove it. But I could make him sweat, and with my next question I succeeded.

"Why do you suppose Janet Maxwell suggested I ask *you* how to find my daughter, Marnie?"

Cain's eyes widened, his jaw dropped. He swiped beads of moisture from above his lip and sputtered his words.

"If you knew Janet Maxwell, then you knew she was crazy. She'd say anything to save herself. You can't be foolish enough to have believed her."

Douglas Cain rose from his chair, adjusted his tie, and buttoned his jacket. He walked around the desk and opened the office door.

"Now if you'll excuse me, Mr. Holt. I have a meeting."

I stood and moved to face him, giving him my most intimidating glare.

"I'm not done with you, counselor."

Douglas Cain was on notice.

***

I hailed a cab and gave the driver my address. As we zigzagged through hordes of Manhattan traffic, my phone vibrated. I smiled when I read the caller's name.

"Maddie."

"Hi, Lucas. I heard what happened with your client. How are you?"

"Honestly, I don't know. I've had some wild cases but..."

"You closed the Rand case. That's a good thing."

"Sure. I'm trying to see it that way. What's going on in Broome?"

"Ha! Nothing much compared to when you were

here. Thank goodness."

"How's work on your house coming along?"

"Great, I've put twenty-five of Broome's unemployed back to work."

"Sounds like a win-win situation."

"We're about to close the case on the two murders. Karen Martin is doing very well, considering."

"Glad to hear it," I said, and I was.

Disappointed the conversation had drifted into business banality, I wondered if it was the right time to suggest we move the relationship to the next level. Maddie beat me to it.

"Listen…" Maddie paused. "Lucas, if you ever need to talk…you know about a case or anything, call me any time."

The softness and sincerity in her voice was as comforting as a favorite blanket.

"Thanks," I said. "I have a few things to wrap up, but how about I call you in a few days and we make a plan for you to visit New York? I'll give you the VIP tour."

"I'd like that, Lucas. But, I'll have to go shopping. I've nothing to wear."

"Perfect."

***

Arriving home, I climbed the stoop and unlocked the front door. The mail was spread across the foyer. I tossed the bills and advertisements on the entrance table and headed for the kitchen.

The refrigerator needed restocking, but I found a

Smithwick's. I grabbed the cold beer and tapped a selection on the wall-mounted keypad of my integrated stereo system. Ella Fitzgerald and Louis Armstrong filled the house with "Summertime."

On my way to collect the mail and go up to my office, I picked up a framed picture of Susan and Marnie taken weeks before she was kidnapped. Looking at their smiling faces made my stomach simultaneously lurch with happiness and wrench in pain. I remembered Maxwell's words. *"You want to know what happened to Marnie. I can tell you."*

Any regrets for shooting Maxwell were interrupted when the doorbell rang. I walked into the adjacent living room and glimpsed out the window. A FedEx truck was at the curb. I opened the door.

"Hi, Mr. Holt. I just need your signature." I signed the electronic device and accepted an express envelope.

"Thanks, Ed." Closing the door, I read the name of the sender: Brown and Harrington, LLC, Attorneys at Law.

Maxwell's lawyers. Was this about the lawsuit she had threatened?

I tore open the envelope. Inside was a picture of a sandy-haired teenage girl with a slight cleft in her chin. Just like mine.

THE END

AUTHORS NOTE:

Thank you for reading *EVERYTHING TO LOSE*. We hope you enjoyed it. Following is an excerpt from book two in the trilogy. We invite you to join Lucas Holt as he continues to unravel the mystery of Marnie's disappearance.

You can visit our website www.jpratto.com for updates on future releases—tentatively set for spring and fall of 2016.

~JP Ratto

SNEAK PEEK

A LUCAS HOLT NOVEL
BOOK TWO

CHAPTER 1

Dr. Robert Vilari stood on the shallow hotel terrace overlooking Uruguay Street, a ten-minute walk from Beirut's central district.

It was early evening and a crush of people was beginning to build along one of the busiest areas in the city. A virtual ghost town by day, soon every café and bar would be filled with tourists and only a few locals. Vilari enjoyed this time of day. The arid, hot air tempered by the setting sun was more bearable, and the blasts of music and laughter from the raucous crowd drowned out the pressures of his job. He sipped his Arak, which he had ordered along with *mezze*, an array of appetizers.

As chief bioengineer for American Defense Laboratories (ADL), he visited overseas chemical plants in countries with liberal corporate laws and "understanding" governments. At one time, he enjoyed hosting lavish parties for power brokers and returning home with an agreement that meant more business for ADL. Now, CEO Mark Halpern asked him to make trips several times a year. Vilari knew, with his heart condition, he needed to cut back. Then he would have to tell Halpern about his health. That wasn't a smart career move.

Swarthy men had in the past offered Vilari money, women, and boys, if he preferred, as incentive to divulge sensitive information. As his personal problems grew, he dreamed of starting over in a new place with his family.

He shut the terrace door, grabbed his wallet, phone, and key card, and left his hotel for another night of mundane networking.

***

Vilari woke to the strong smell of dokha tobacco, with a massive headache and the need to urinate. With one hand over his eyes to block the light streaming into the room, he slid his legs over the side of the bed. He sat up and jerked, startled by the olive-skinned stranger relaxed in a chair, staring at him as he inhaled from a carved medwakh. First surprised and then angry, he was too weak to mount a verbal attack. Vilari vaguely remembered him from the night before. He moved to stand, as the man looked on, seemingly assessing his condition. Vilari shook off the penetrating stare and stepped toward the bathroom, losing his equilibrium. He attempted to straighten but fell backwards onto the bed.

The stranger, tall and thin, rose to pick up a glass from a room service cart. He turned back to Vilari. "I am Amari Abboud," he said, handing Vilari a milky beverage. "Drink it slowly. We have a lot to talk about."

Vilari swallowed and cleared his throat. "What do you want?"

Settling back into the chair, Abboud pulled an envelope from his pocket. He began shuffling through several photographs then glanced at Vilari, who winced at the taste of the drink and rubbed his stomach. "Despite how you feel now, you had a good night." Abboud held up a photo of a woman straddled atop Vilari, her smooth, bronzed back to the camera. "Yes, a very good night."

He threw the photos on the bed. With a shaky hand, Vilari spread them apart and gasped. In one, the woman had her face buried in his groin. Another showed Vilari returning the favor. He gagged and fell to his knees, grabbing a small wastebasket. He retched violently. Exhausted, he remained on the floor and leaned against the bed. Abboud tossed Vilari a hand towel to wipe the vomit from his mouth.

"Feel better?" Abboud asked.

With tears sliding down his blanched face, Vilari blinked.

"Good." Amari Abboud said. "Let's begin…"

***

Standing in the foyer of my Gramercy Park brownstone, I stared at the envelope addressed to me, Lucas Holt PI, which had held a photo sent by a previous client.

After receiving the photograph from Janet Maxwell's attorneys, my initial shock had turned to guarded optimism. My first inclination was to call my ex-wife, Susan, and share the hope that the girl in the photo was Marnie.

Fifteen years before, during the investigation of a sensitive case, my six-month-old daughter was abducted from a daycare center. At the time, I was an NYPD detective looking into the murder of a call girl with ties to a New York state senator. I always believed the two incidents were connected.

The idea Marnie was still alive and we could be a family again rushed through my mind and made my heart pump faster. However, Susan's remarriage to Jim O'Brien was a major obstacle.

I procrastinated with the excuse that I didn't want to offer Susan any false hope. Truth be told, I was afraid to raise any within myself. Once I spoke aloud to anyone about the photo—about finding Marnie, I would have the expectation of her recovery. With no new cases on my plate, I wouldn't let anything distract me from searching for my daughter. I only had to decide when to tell Susan.

The decision was taken out of my hands when I received a phone call from Susan's husband telling me she was in hospice.

***

I'd spent my fair share of time in hospitals before my parents died. They both had suffered terminal illnesses, two years apart, and when they were near their end, I'd gone back home to be with them. The only occasion where I didn't dread entering a medical facility was when my daughter Marnie was born. Her birth was one of the happiest moments of my life, her disappearance the worst.

I drove to Middletown, N.Y. to visit Susan. More like hotel than hospital, her room was large and comfortably furnished for guests. The hospital bed, though, was a bleak reminder of her illness. No lights were on, and half-closed shades blocked the late afternoon sun. Shadows of low-hanging tree branches outside the windows danced on the floor like dark, tentacled marionettes.

As I drew up to the side of the bed, Susan shifted her head toward me. Her eyes eased open, halfway and then wide with recognition. She lifted a gaunt, pale hand. I enclosed it in mine and she smiled.

"Lucas," she whispered, "so glad to see you."

I tried to speak, but the words wouldn't pass the lump in my throat. I sat in the chair beside the bed, holding her hand. Gently. Then I brought it to my lips and kissed it. The disease had drained Susan's body of its warmth. I held on, wishing I could transmit some of my own health and energy through her iced skin.

Oh God, seeing her this way is so hard.

"I just found out," I said. "I've been meaning to call you."

She summoned enough strength to squeeze my hand. "It's okay. You're a busy man." She licked her parched lips and swallowed. "You've helped a lot of people."

It was a compliment, but all I could hear were the words she neglected to say. *Why couldn't you help us?*

"Susan, I have something to show you. I've

struggled the last few weeks with whether or not I should. I don't want to upset you. Not that it will be upsetting. I'm just not sure."

She squeezed my hand again so I would stop fumbling over my words. She knew me well and had always scolded me for beating around the bush when I had something to tell her. Good or bad.

"What is it, Lucas? You can see...I don't have all day." She smiled at the joke, but neither of us laughed, and I watched a tear slide down her cheek. My stomach clenched.

I can't bear this.

I released her hand, inhaled deeply, and coughed to clear my throat. Then I pulled out the photo of the girl with the cleft chin, just like mine, who also had Susan's small, patrician nose and soft brown eyes.

Susan stared at the picture of the young girl I held in front of her. I watched her face and swore I could see the emotions that had surged through me pass over her as well.

She took the photo from me into her shaking hand. "Turn on the light," she said. "Oh my God, Lucas. I need to see her in the light."

No longer in shadows, some of the gloom left me. Susan lay transfixed on the face in the photo.

"It's her, isn't it?" she finally asked.

"I believe it is. By the way, you were right about her eyes. They did turn brown."

Susan raised her brow and pursed her lips, giving me the familiar, "Of course I was right" look. Then she turned serious. "Where is she?"

I had to tell her, "I don't know."

I briefly relayed the circumstances of how I came to possess the photo. Susan let it slip from her hands to rest over her heart, closed her eyes, and wept. I wept too.

***

Not wanting to be anywhere else, the time passed more easily than I'd thought. The sun had set, and the room grew chilly. Slouched with my legs stretched and my head rested on the back of a chair, an odd peacefulness warmed me. After a while, Susan drifted off to sleep. I moved to take back the picture when she woke.

"Can you leave it here?" she asked.

I hadn't even thought about it. It was the only one I had. I asked an attendant if there was somewhere to make a copy for Susan. It wouldn't be great, but it would do.

We looked again at the image of who we both accepted was our daughter. Susan's breathing became labored. My visit had been too much for her. I leaned over and kissed her on the lips.

"I love you, Susan." I wouldn't say goodbye.

She didn't return the sentiment although her eyes held the look I'd seen long ago that told me so. It was enough. I turned to leave when she grabbed my hand with such force it startled me.

"Find her, Lucas," she said, her voice strong and commanding. "Find her."

ACKNOWLEDGEMENTS

We wish to thank all who, with their knowledge and encouragement, contributed to the writing of this book. Thank you to our children, family, and friends, who are our built-in fan base and cheerleaders. Thanks to the members of Abacoa Writers and Creative Writers of Abacoa for their critical feedback and their friendship. Thank you to Rob L. Bacon of The Perfect Write for his invaluable manuscript critique. Our gratitude goes to the Limitless Publishing team for their technical expertise and creative talent.

I would like to acknowledge Hofstra University's Continuing Education Writing Program, where I began honing my craft. Thank you to children's author Brian Heinz, whose "noun rich, verb rich" mantra helped me to become a better writer. Warm thanks to Gina Shaw, Lois Kipnis, Barbara Senenman, and Shanna Silva: writers, editors, and friends, who have shared my journey from the beginning. Thanks to my mom Muriel Stapleton for her love and strength. A most special thank you to my husband Pete, who always took the time to read and edit my work and provide sound advice and unyielding love and support.

~J.R.

In writing this story, I drew upon the sum of many experiences. Thanks to my parents and my sister, all who have passed, who shaped, molded, and nurtured my personal credo, "Attitude is rule one." Thanks go to the US Navy and US Marine Corps who taught me strength of character, independence, and to focus on goals and achieve them. Loving thanks to my wife Judy, who has always been there for me.

~*P.R.*

ABOUT THE AUTHORS

JP Ratto is a husband and wife collaborative writing team. *EVERYTHING TO LOSE* is the first of a three-book series featuring private investigator Lucas Holt.

Judy began writing full time six years ago. She attended Hofstra University's Writing Intensive in the summer of 2010, and participated in a Hofstra-sponsored writing and critique group from 2009 to 2012. She has written an upper middle-grade fantasy adventure and a children's mystery chapter book. Judy also does free-lance editing.

Pete Ratto, a former member of the U.S. Navy serving half his enlistment with the U.S. Marine Corp, is a retired corporate accountant and is now writing full time.

Both are avid readers of mysteries, thrillers and suspense. Active in a critique group made up of local authors, they enjoy discussions on all aspects of the craft of writing. Pete enjoys photography, writing and going to the beach. In her spare time, Judy paints watercolors and to her husband's delight, cooks an occasional dinner. They have a son and a daughter, both grown and living in New York. Pete and Judy live in southern Florida with their cat, Gillian.

Facebook:
https://www.facebook.com/jp.ratto.1

Twitter:
https://twitter.com/jandpratto

Website:
www.jpratto.com

Made in the USA
San Bernardino, CA
18 December 2015